MEATING DALTON
DANIELS DUET
BOOK TWO

MAE K. KNIGHT

Copyright © 2024 by Mae K. Knight

Print ISBN

979-8-3305-2747-2

Meating Dalton

https://maeknight.carrd.co/

Written by: Mae K. Knight

Cover design: Artista Gráfico

Editing: Stacey's Bookcorner Editing Service

Proofreading: Stacey's Bookcorner Editing Service

All rights reserved.

Please respect the author and do not participate in or encourage piracy of copyrighted materials that would violate the author's rights.

No part of this book may be reproduced in any form or by any electronic or mechanical means, including information storage and retrieval systems, without written permission from the author, except for the use of brief quotations in a book review.

No AI was used in any part of the creation of this book. The author also doesn't give permission for anyone to upload their books, covers, or commissioned art to AI training sites.

The unauthorized reproduction or distribution of a copyrighted work is illegal. Criminal copyright infringement, including infringement without monetary gain, is investigated by the FBI and is punishable by up to five years in federal prison and a fine of $250,000

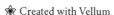 Created with Vellum

ALSO BY MAE K. KNIGHT

LASHER BROTHERS DUET

Surviving Zaine

Escaping Xavier

Lasher Brothers Duet: The Complete Duet

DANIELS DUET

Claiming Sarah

Meating Dalton

Daniels Duet: The Complete Duet

CHAOTIC COUSINS DUET

Chasing Deaton

Hunting Killian

SINS OF THE LASHER FAMILY

Keeping Xavier

Xavier

TABOO TALES

Daddy's Girl

Call Me Weirdo

Tempting Uncle Maddox

Resisting My Brother
Still Daddy's Girl
Catch Me, Freak

CONTENTS

Meating Dalton	1
Trigger Warnings	3
Prologue	7
1. Death & A Funeral	9
2. Unlucky Prey	13
3. Black	18
4. Goddess Meat	26
5. Sisters	32
6. Temptation	38
7. Midnight Snack	46
8. The Other Woman	52
9. Run	59
10. Secrets	64
11. Meating Dalton	71
12. The Task	75
13. Ladies First	82
14. A Bath	86
15. The Show	90
16. Call Me Dalton	94
17. Parents	100
18. Mistakes	108
19. Morning After	114
20. Fix It	119
21. Space	125
22. Claiming Zaiden	130
23. Finding Family	134
24. My Flower	141
Epilogue	144
About the Author	151

MEATING DALTON

Everyone is meat.

    My foster parents.

    The neighbor's dog.

My biological parents who abandoned me.

I do not care that they put me up for adoption.

I care that they picked the wrong twin to keep.

So they must die.

To be filleted or not to be filleted, as Shakespeare said.

And they will be as soon as I find someone who knows where they are.

Natalia Bell, social worker extraordinaire, knows. So I take her.

But this little flower has thorns, each prick causing new *feelings* to sprout.

I'll have to kill her before she does something crazy, like make me fall in love with her.

And what of this Jokester twin of mine? Will he feel the sting of my blade?

Can *love* stall my hand from slitting Natalia's pretty little throat?

Find out on the next episode of Chef's Kiss.

TRIGGER WARNINGS

This book contains sensitive material relating to:

Adoption
Animal death (off page)
Blood/Gore/Violence/Mutilation
Cannibalism
Cheating (Not between MCs)
Corpse dismemberment
Dub-con/Non-con
Emotional and Verbal Child Abuse
Explicit Language
Explicit Sex Scenes
Facial disfigurement (not MMC)
Fertility issues (lightly touched on)
Forcible nonconsensual ingestion of bodily fluids (piss)
Kidnapping
Murder
Parental Death
Period (blood) Play
Physical child abuse (starvation, locking in a closet)

Pregnancy (not FMC)
Reverse Age gap
Somnophilia
Stalking
Torture

I highly recommend you take these triggers seriously, particularly the ones relating to graphic on-page torture. It is not for the faint of heart and Dalton isn't meant to be a redeemable character. Happy reading.

DEDICATION

You read the title.
You saw the blurb.
You know what you're in for, you naughty, naughty piece of meat.
Mhm. Delicious, sweet meat.
Will you taste as good as my flower?
Well, will you?
Because one of us will be dying for me to taste you.

PROLOGUE

DALTON

"*One, two, three,*" *I count out loud, hands clasped to my eyes and face pressed into the wall of a pitch dark closet. I'm scared, but I didn't tell Mom that. She never wanted to play with me before.*

We're playing hide and seek. She's hiding while I count. I don't know why I had to be in the closet. I don't like it.

"Done!" I shout, dropping my hands. My chest hurts, like when I run outside during playtime. I shuffle in the dark toward the door. I'm scared, really scared.

"Mom!" I cry, pulling on the doorknob. It won't turn. Why won't it turn? Did she lock it?

"Mom!" Tears spill down my face. Dad says big boys don't cry, but it's dark in here. I don't like the dark. It feels like someone's in here with me, breathing down my neck. Dad says there's no such thing as monsters, but it feels like a fib, like when Johnny pushed me down while we were playing and told the teacher I fell.

"Mom, please!" My forehead thumps into the door and something moves behind me.

"No, no. Not real. Dad says you're not real." My fist bang on

the door, hoping the noise will drown out the monster in the closet with me.

"Mommy!" I know she hates it when I call her that. Her lips would turn down and she'd pretend she didn't hear me, even though I sometimes see her glance at me when I say it.

When I hear footsteps outside the door, I stop crying, and wipe my face in case it's Dad. When they stop at the door, I curl my hands, waiting for one of my parents to open the door. Maybe Mom's punishing me. But I don't know what I did wrong.

"Mom?" What if the monster slid beneath the door to the other side? That can't happen. Or at least I think it can't, but Santa finds a way in.

The footsteps start to move away. No, no. I shake my head and bang my fist on the door again.

"Mom!" Snot and tears drip down my face. I don't care about being a big boy. I want out. Out. Out. Out.

"Please let me out! I'll be good!" I promise, hoping she's listening. She doesn't answer me and I slide to the floor with my cheek pressed to the door. She's not coming. I don't know what I did wrong.

Maybe if I can't see the monster, then it's not there. Wrapping my arms around my knees, I bury my face in them. I stay like that, whispering over and over, "It's not real. I'm alone. It's not real."

I don't know how long I stay like that, but it feels like a long time before Dad pulls open the closet and carries me to bed. He doesn't say anything about the dried tears and snot. I'm glad. I really tried to be a big boy.

DEATH & A FUNERAL

DALTON

ONE

"We're gathered here today for the dearly departed…"

A priest drones on, his voice sounding like buzzing insects. Or maybe that's the whispers of the congregation. Or the sizzling of my skin. Surely, a sinner like myself should burst into flames instead of calmly sitting on a church pew.

A woman keens loudly in the back of the church. Her wailful moans carrying toward me and making my palms itch to slide a blade into it and permanently silence her fucking fake crying. Nobody misses Charles Lewis that much, not even the secretary he fucked regularly, who sits near the casket with silent crocodile tears sliding down her made-up face. Must be top dollar make-up to not smudge or look out of place.

Out of the corner of my eyes, I spot black nail polish catching the light streaming in from the stained glass. My cousin, Deaton, rests a hand on my bouncing knee. I hadn't realized my entire body's buzzing with activity.

My other cousin, Rhys, lounges lazily on my left, arms

crossed over his chest. He doesn't bother touching me. He knows better and Deaton foolishly trusts I won't skin him in the middle of my adoptive father's funeral service. Charles Lewis tolerated me. And I'm barely tolerating this stuffy, tight suit that covers nearly every inch of skin. Maybe Aunt Shirley thought everyone would mistake me for the Grim Reaper with my skeletal tattoo stretching from the tips of my fingers to just below my jaw and that's why she insisted on the suit.

Would Deaton miss his mother if I killed her?

"Quit fucking fidgeting," he snaps in my ear. I gnash my teeth at him, regretting allowing him to confiscate my knives. Maybe he knows me better than I give him credit for. Either fucking way, I'm done with the droning and buzzing and wailing of sheep. Any more of it and I'll really shock everyone by throwing the casket wide open, jumping into it, and peeling the flesh from dear old Charles. It'd be a bitch with rigor mortis toughening the skin.

"I'm out of here," I growl at my cousin, body poised to jump out of the pew. Pain lances my wrist and I look down to see the fucker pulled one of my blades out of his pocket and made a superficial cut through the folded down cuffs at my wrist. Blood wells and makes my stomach grumble. Immediately, I want a rare steak, licking my lips at the blood.

"Your ass is staying until they throw fucking dirt on the casket. I am not," Deaton growls, "covering for you if you bail cause your head ain't screwed on tight. If Rhys and I have to suffer through this service then so do you. Now, be fucking still." Metal glints then the blade gets stowed back into my cousin's pocket. Oh, sure, he gets to have a weapon, but I'm not trusted with one.

Ears burning at the tongue lashing and feeling like a

damn child that got its ass spanked, I huff back into my seat, crossing my arms to emulate Rhys. His lips curl out of the corner of my eyes and he too is lucky I'm unarmed. I'd give his pretty boy face a permanent damn smile. Deaton's nail polish gleam as he tugs on his cuffs unnecessarily.

How the fuck did I get saddled with Hollywood and Metalhead for cousins? The world truly isn't fair.

"Another!" I slur, slamming a shot glass down onto damp, varnished wood. Rhys' baby blues look me up and down critically and with a sigh, he refills my glass. Smoke drifts from the lit end of Deaton's cigarette.

"You should really cut him off," he tells his cousin. My cousin? My head shakes, sloshing liquid around. Whatever. We're somebody's cousins.

"His dad died. I think he's entitled to get trashed. And its fun to watch him slow down. Always bouncing around like he's doing coke," Rhys complains. My dad died? A laugh bubbles from me. I suppose he did but if we're talking biological, then I don't know that fucker. No, Charles took that information with him to the grave and not even his solicitor would tell me who my birth parents were.

"I should go find my dad. Make him pay," I say but the words traveling to my ears sound funny, like I said them too fast. Rhys chuckles, shaking his head and causing blonde hair to brush his forehead. Deaton snorts and more smoke wafts my way. I look around the barely lit bar, taking in the gyrating bodies on the dance floor, flashing strobe lights, and the inconspicuous bouncers stationed in odd corners. Rhys must really like people to own and manage a bar. That or he's a masochist cause he always looks constipated when he's interacting with people that aren't paying patrons.

"Pay for giving me up," I mumble, rediscovering my original train of thought. Cunt Samantha—my dead foster mother—never told me the name of my birth parents either. No, she merely taunted me with the knowledge that I was unwanted and an abomination. I wish I could revisit the euphoria of slitting her throat and silencing her for good. Maybe I'll see her in the next life.

Another laugh stumbles from my numb lips. Why are they numb?

"Let it go, Zac. It's in the past," Deaton says, smoke spilling from his mouth and nostrils. Some of it snakes down my throat, spurring a coughing fit. A large hand slams into my back, trying to force the smoke out.

"Damn," I groan. "Don't ever give me fucking CPR. You'll crack my ribs beating on my chest like you just did to my back." Rhys laughs, even white teeth catching the light. They think I'm joking. About my biological parents, that is.

But for too long the thought simmered in my mind. Where are they? Was Samantha right? There's only one way to find the answers I seek and that's by cutting it out of them.

And I don't mean that figuratively.

"Mazel tov, Charles," I whisper into the rim of my glass, downing the whiskey back in one motion. I hope you're enjoying Hell, you old bastard.

UNLUCKY PREY

DALTON

TWO

My skin itches and I fight the urge to claw at it until it bleeds, red painting the black and white ink decorating my skin. From suffering emerges the strongest souls or whatever some dead fuck said. I must suffer to get what I want and what I want is to cut open my biological parents until their insides spill out, along with the reason for why they gave me up.

It doesn't bother me. I'm beyond such trivial issues. Some adopted kids wonder why, wallowing in their self-pity. Oh, no. I'm comfortable with who I am. I'm Zachary fucking Dalton Lewis, who enjoys spending the Lewis' money at his leisure.

What I didn't enjoy was the meat sack that was my adoptive mother, Samantha Lewis or Charles Lewis, who's worm food now. I wish I could say I'm responsible for both of their fates, but can only lay claim to one. I'd have killed Charles too if he hadn't tolerated my existence and made half-assed attempts to care for my needs.

My nails drag along the length of my pants, hands needing to do something other than sliding down to my ankles, pulling a knife free and stabbing into chatty Becky's chest, who's sitting in the creaky plastic chair next to me. Why the fuck do they make these chairs so small and what's up with the magazines?

No, I don't give a fuck about flu season. I'm sitting in the waiting room of the adoption agency that handled my case because I'm looking for a referral for a urologist. Are some dicks really that small? My hands are half tempted to pick up the pamphlet on testicular cancer just to compare sizes. Those guys are advertising for the wrong health issue.

"Lewis!" A clear, feminine voice calls out and I abandon my disgruntlement with the entertainment options. It's showtime. Rising from my claustrophobic seat, I brush imaginary lint away, tugging on my cuffs. A collar digs into the sensitive skin of my neck but I ignore it, striding over to the smiling receptionist.

Brown pupils widen, drifting up and down my form. Black suits me, absorbing the light and conveniently hiding blood stains when necessary. It's my second favorite color after red. For blood, duh.

I flash a dimpled smile at—a quick glance at a name badge sporting a blurry photo—Amanda. Her brown roots override the blonde streaks through her hair, contrasting with the tale the badge tells. Not my problem.

Leaning over the polished counter, the scent of lemon polish floating on the air, I lower my lids, letting them drift into a half-hooded look. Females eat that shit up.

"Hi. I'm Zachary Lewis. I was wondering if I could peek at my adoption file," I belt out smoothly, keeping my smile firmly in place. Red stains Amanda's skin as she shoots a flustered look from me to the computer in front of her. Deft fingers fly over keyboards, each jab stabbing into my sensitive earlobes.

God, why can't I kill her and pull up the information myself?

Oh, right, that's "illegal". So is intentional starvation but that never stopped Samantha or me from slitting her throat. I smile at the memory while waiting for Amanda to pull up my information. She *harrumphs* softly, sliding a cautious look my way. I lock onto it.

Reading prey is a skill I fostered and nurtured. They disgust me but studying them is a necessary evil. All the better to kill you, my dear.

"Problem?" I ask in a smooth voice. She mumbles slightly before clearing her slender throat. It begs for my knives.

"Actually, yours is a closed adoption. I'm not allowed to disclose details," she mutters in an apologetic tone, avoiding my glare. It's the dumbest shit I've ever heard. But I can't tell her that. Charles Lewis prided himself on his ability to conduct business in the middle of the most improbable conditions. I channel my adopted father's ghost, loathing the slimy feeling coating my skin.

"Of course. I understand you're doing your job. But this is such a personal issue for me." My lips pull down into a grimace, insincere eyes lowering to shield the hard glint that whisper "I want to see your insides".

"Could you possibly tell me who worked the case? I'd love to hear whatever stories they have to tell, to make me feel closer to my parents." I bat my lashes, and flash only a half of my dimpled smile.

Dark pupils expand, invading the brown irises. A pulse throbs in her throat, a throat I'd love to slice cleanly across with the blades hidden beneath my clothing. That's it, take the bait. My tattoos end just below my jawline, lining my throat. But my face remains unblemished, luring prey into a false sense of safety.

My smile says "I'm safe" and "I'd never dream of hurting you." Fucking idiots. Never trust a pretty face or a smile. But people don't listen to their elders anymore and all the better for me. Amanda returns her eyes to her computer, pressing buttons in a rapid pattern and a whirring sound starts up behind her.

Dark hair whips forward before falling to rest against her back as she hastens to the printer, slender fingers pulling my documents free. White teeth nibble at soft lips. I'm close to losing her. I feel it slipping from my fingers like vapors of smoke. I need her more than she needs me.

My instincts burrow deep, grasping at ages old acting lessons. Tears swell and I temporarily wonder when the last time I genuinely cried was. It's too late for such thoughts now. One fat droplet falls, landing on the swirling streaks of brown in the marble countertop.

"Oh, my God," a soft sympathetic voice intones. I fight the smile wanting to curve my lips. It's not about the pleasure of luring prey. It's the hunt, the chase, the search for the truth. That's all I need, to know who my parents were and why they gave me up. If they won't willingly tell me, I'll cut it from them.

Simple. Easy. Uncomplicated. It's how I operate best.

But I must play the game, lifting the mask from my face while still shielding my true nature behind layers of civility. I despise it but it's more than a necessary evil. It's survival.

"I just don't know what I'll do if I don't find out more about them," I whisper, letting tears leak free and slide down my cheeks. The blatant display of weakness sinks into me, gnawing into my tender, fleshy layers. A true predator would never stoop to this level, it whispers. I want to jam a knife into the imagined throat of my inner monologue. I detest it.

But the time isn't right to eliminate all traces of my adoptive mother and father's essence. It permeates every atom of my being. I can't peel back enough skin to root out the source.

Amanda whimpers softly, paper sliding across the marble countertop.

"You didn't get this from me. They're just names, the names of everyone that worked on your case. I can't tell you more." Her voice fades into a soft, pathetic whisper. Sincerity lances me. My defenses deflect the carefully targeted blow. The cute brunette tried and failed to slide beneath my defenses. They remain resolutely closed. Just like she shouldn't trust a predator, I'd never trust prey.

"Thank you, Amanda," I whisper softly, keeping my eyes downcast. It's easier to hide the madness this way. Her fingers slide across one of my tattooed hands. Unmarred flesh contrasts entirely too nicely with the ivory bones painted on my skin.

Damn. She shouldn't have touched me. Pity, I was considering letting her live past this encounter. How sad that it just might be Amanda's day to die and she doesn't know it yet. It's fucking unlucky. For her. Sucks to be meat, I guess.

BLACK

DALTON

THREE

Well, no one ever said piss smells lovely. A clear container holding a substantial amount of urine the color of hay rests next to another container filled with congealed pig's blood. A smile pulls at my lips, leaning my head back and letting the soothing notes of Bach wash over me, chasing away the restless energy that's dogged me for days now. Amanda's list proved fruitful, and I fought a simmering rage upon discovering my late adopted father's solicitor on the list.

Turning my back on the table housing my cooking ingredients, I face Jacobson Black. Bound with rope tethering him to a chair, he appears frail, sickly even. My upper lip curls at the idea of feasting on cancerous meat. Too busy following his every move for the past three days, I haven't found time to check his health records. Oh, well.

If I had dogs, he'd make a hearty meal for them. My bare feet slap tile, approaching the unconscious older man.

Wrinkles line his face, and gray streaks pepper his hair. Looks like he's led a long, hard life. How fortunate it's about to end.

A slap shatters the quiet in between transitions, mournful notes chasing the echo. Shaking out my stinging hand, I glare at Jacobson, watching his eyes slowly blink to life. Shaggy furrowed brows cause his wrinkles to deepen. My smile stretches wide as he begins the predictable routine of tugging on the restraints, mouth opening and closing in shock. Mock innocence paints my face, concealing my rage that rises with the crescendo of the music.

"Hello, again, Mr. Black. I was hoping we could revisit the topic of my birth parents." My lips morph from a smile, setting the tone of the evening. I played nice and asked politely after my father's funeral for details about my adoption. He gave me nearly the same spiel as the adoption agency. Knives find their way into my hands, as familiar as a lover's caress.

No shirt dons my torso. A harness crisscrosses my chest, leather sheaths lovingly holding my beloveds.

I want his blood to stain my fucking skin as I carve the truth out of his traitorous, weak body.

"Start talking, Mr. Black, before I lose the little patience God saw fit to bless me with," I sneer at the elderly man.

"Mr. Lewis, please. I can't—" His denial ends in a high-pitched scream, blood welling around the point of the knife I stabbed straight into his right leg. It does precious little to calm me. I am tired of *waiting* for pathetic people to design to tell me the truth about where I come from. The knowledge should've been gifted to me long before now.

Mr. Black gets to suffer from both sets of parents' lack of insight into how I'd cope with being left in the dark.

Left in the dark.

"Please let me out! I'll be good!"

No, that bitch is dead. I bury the other blade into Mr. Black's other leg. His squeal tickles my ear, urging me to do more damage, to disappear into the alluring embrace of bloodlust. I step back, letting air sweep into my chest. It heaves up and down as I'm caught in the pendulum of the past and present.

Darkness pressing in on all sides, choking the life from my lungs.

Blindly, I stumble toward the container of golden liquid, snatching up a funnel in the other hand.

"Please," Mr. Black weeps, sounding like the bitch that bleated like a fucking sheep during the funeral. If Deaton and Rhys hadn't hemmed me in on both sides, I'd have found her after the burial and granted her wish of seeing Charles again.

"Quit whining. You're giving me a headache and I can't decide what side dish you'd go better with. How do you feel about mashed potatoes and gravy?" I ask nonchalantly, forcing my breathing to calm. We've barely gotten started.

His wrinkled, turtle neck swivels left and right, the movement agitating the rest of his body. Blood drips in a steady trail, pooling beneath the chair. Licking my lips, I walk back toward my prey. Maybe if he used his brain to tell me what I want to know, he could save himself some pain. He doesn't know he's already dead.

Dead man walking, Mr. Black. Say hi to Death for me.

"Listen. I googled recipes. And the consensus is you need something acidic to tenderize meat. The pH of urine is between four and eight. So I figured I'd save money by using mine." Jacobson folds in on himself, surrendering to deep, wracking sobs. Maybe if Samantha paid more attention to my tears, I'd have more sympathy for the crying of others.

His weeping is fucking with the vibe Bach is setting. Classical music, tenderizing meat, getting answers to long sought after questions. It should be a great fucking night. I should feel euphoric instead of edgy, body twitching with a whirlpool of emotions. Giving up on untangling the thread of bundled feelings, I sink into what I do best.

Meat meet hunter. Let's make dinner.

"Well, looks like we're doing this the hard way." It's his only warning before I transfer the funnel to under my arm, slip another blade free and use it pin his testicles to the chair. The scream he releases would make a soprano jealous. I use the opportunity of his mouth being gaped open to shove the funnel nearly to the back of his fucking throat. While he's gagging around it, I pour the acrid liquid into the funnel.

His body convulses, and I jerk back in time for him to vomit all over his lap. Tears, snot, and blood mingle into a nasty stench, curdling my appetite. Fuck eating him. He's going to be barbecue for some wild animals.

"Morgan Daniels," he croaks from a raw and probably burning throat. My head tilts, silently urging him to spill the rest of the tale everyone thinks is best kept from me.

"Her father tasked me with managing her conservatorship. She was gravely, mentally ill. And pregnant with twins. I thought it was a mercy letting her keep just one. Charles and Samantha tried for years to conceive…" The rest of his raspy words slip through my ear canals and back out.

Twins. Only kept one.

The world spins, the opposite of a funhouse mirror. I'm the fucking clown in this circus. The one given away.

I don't remember acting. My mind just blanks and I'm suddenly staring into the grisly, brutally shredded chest cavity of Jacobson Black, letting two knives slip from limp fingers. Red tints everything.

Sinking to the floor, surrounded by piss, vomit and blood, I can't help but think this is the biggest fuck you from the universe. My own chest feels just as ravaged as Mr. Black's. I did nothing to deserve this.

"I'm not your mother! Quit calling me that, abomination!" Her words filter through my brain on a loop.

Pick one. Keep one.

Maybe Samantha was right and Morgan Daniels sensed it when she held my twin to her breast, letting Jacobson ferry me away. I hope they're all still living. My only regret tonight is killing Mr. Black before I could get a location from him. But rest assured, Daniels' family.

I'm fucking coming for you.

Burnt flesh saturates the air, snaking down my nostrils to cause a Texas sized migraine. Or maybe that's from carting the one hundred plus pound carcass of Jacobson Black from the trunk of one of the cars I inherited from my father's passing to the woods surrounding Rhys' cabin. The ex-navy seal enjoys living outside the boundaries of society.

And I like taking advantage of the seclusion to burn bodies behind my cousin's home. It's a win-win for everyone. He doesn't mind the smell and he's probably out managing his bar.

Twigs snap under heavy footsteps and I don't turn around, watching the flames lick at Mr. Black's corpse, consuming his meat to feed the hungry fire. Shapes dance and writhe in the mesmerizing light, lulling me from the thoughts taunting my brain.

"I thought I'd find you here," Deaton says, smoke spilling from his mouth to float in my line of sight. The fucker is going to choke and die on a cigarette one day. I can't summon any remorse over the potential demise. He made his coffin, fully prepared to lie in it when his time comes.

I hope I'm as *laissez-faire* when it's my turn to meet the reaper. For now, Death doesn't bother me. It's an everyday occurrence, a sentence I mete out to others. I wasn't even present when Charles' heart gave out, cock at half mast inside his young mistress.

Is she really a mistress if his wife has been dead for over five years?

"Tell me what's going through your head, Zac. Cause whoever the fuck you're burning smells fucking awful." I bark out a weak laugh, tears stinging my eyes. Deaton's right. Jacobson smells like fetid meat. Not even wolves would want to dine on his cold flesh once the flames die down.

I didn't even get to marinate him in pig's blood. He died too quickly, frail body giving out beneath my flurry of strikes, sharp metal tearing through tender flesh. The memory superimposes itself in my mind, but I still barely recall slipping the knives from their sheaths.

One minute he's breathing, croaking his way through a tale I wasn't prepared to hear and in the next he's dead.

"I'm fine. You can go. Unless Rhys sent you out here." I doubt the veteran called Deaton. No, my cousin possesses an unnatural sixth sense of when I'm dancing near the edge of the abyss. It mocks me, whispering for me to jump in, that it'll numb all of my problems.

But it can't rewind time to convince Morgan Daniels I'm worth keeping. It's the albatross looped around my neck, choking any air I manage to inhale.

"She was wrong, Zac." Deaton doesn't elaborate, but he doesn't need to. Ten years older, but he's caught flashes of the dark side of his aunt Samantha, the side she hid from her husband before I killed her.

How does he know that it's *her* haunting me and not Charles?

Maybe because Charles never locked me in closets or withheld food from me.

I'd be dead if not for Deaton. One day, he took one look at the bones protruding through my skin and insisted I have dinner at his house with his parents. Despite anticipating a cruel trick from Samantha, I agreed, tear-stained and pleading with my mother to let me go with him. She only agreed after Uncle Dick promised to keep me for the night, giving her a reprieve from my presence.

Deaton's pity used to sour my stomach and make my skin itch. Instead, gratitude stings my insides because he saved me that night. Who knew how many more missed meals my young body could take before it gave out?

Samantha Lewis certainly didn't give a fuck.

I could never repay him, even if I despise the leash he pulls taut around me from time to time. I'd kill for the fucker. I just hope he doesn't make me bury him in his emo damn clothing. Black is my color.

Remembering his off-hand but spot on comment, I open my mouth.

"Maybe. Or maybe she was right. Maybe if she hadn't behaved the way she did, I wouldn't have turned into a monster. Either way, we won't know now, will we?" Pulling my eyes from the dancing streaks of light, I lock onto my cousin. Sharp, defined facial features catch the inconsistent light. It brightens brown eyes to a beautiful hazel.

"I guess we're both monsters then," he remarks in a bored tone, head turning to lock eyes with me. Emotion rarely swims in the brown depths, and I never appreciated it more than I do now. I couldn't stand his pity tonight. He hides it pretty damn well, but in the earlier days, it bled through nearly every selfless act.

He's the literal fucking wind beneath my wings. Blinking, I avoid the eyes that see too much. Numb lips move, spilling the poison in my veins.

"I won't rest until they're dead, D. I can't. I need to do this." My voice cracks only slightly and in typical Deaton fashion, he doesn't question me further. In my peripheral, I catch his head moving up and down, a lit cigarette held between his lips.

Together, we stare into the flames, watching it burn away my sin. If only it could do it for every one of them. Tonight, I'll take the win and tomorrow, I'll resume the hunt.

Morgan Daniels owes me some fucking answers.

GODDESS MEAT

DALTON

FOUR

"Have you given it a rest yet?" Deaton asks after taking a sip from his bottle of beer. Another week slipped past me while I hunted down the names on the list. Todd Peterson is next but he's out of the fucking country for the next two months. I could always catch a flight to wherever he's at but would that be too extreme?

But I don't answer my cousin, staring down into my glass of whiskey as I ponder my next move. I wish killing everyone at the adoption agency was a viable option for fucking refusing to tell me anything. Thank the man upstairs for weak-willed women. Amanda truly did go down well with a glass of wine.

The next best option to slaughtering the employees at the agency would be eliminating whoever invented closed adoptions, making it illegal to disclose details, even to the individuals involved.

What kind of dumb shit is that? Don't I have a right to know where the fuck I come from?

"You need to get laid," my cousin chirps. Scowling, I

shoot him a glare that he ignores with a smirk. The weird fuck is always harping on about me getting my dick wet. As if. I don't fuck animals. Turning from him to glance at the patrons of the bar we're at, I try to see what he sees.

Not that he's getting any pussy, either. The fucker is bored. Bored with life, bored with killing and bored with women. He needs a new damn hobby, to hang up his hat as the *Heartbreaker* killer.

Music pumps from speakers spaced throughout the establishment. Recessed lights flash intermittently. Black lacquer walls help shield the extracurricular activities of some of the drunk animals present.

They're all animals. To be killed, to be skinned and to be eaten. The end.

Why would I want to put my dick in any one of them?

A hand lands on my shoulder and I debate the logistics of removing it without spilling any blood on my all black clothing. His other hand enters my line of sight and points to my right, guiding my eyes to a wall of flesh facing us.

"Her," he coaxes. Lights shimmer off mocha skin, and it ripples with the woman's movements. Her dress exposes her entire back, even the dip above where her round ass starts. I have to admit, it's a nice ass.

My stomach sours at the thought, and I push Deaton away, jumping to my feet. He laughs and I realize the gothic fucker is amusing himself at my expense. Even white teeth gleam and kohl lined brown eyes sparkle with mirth. Narrowing my eyes on him, I decide to play.

It's not like I have much else to do. More than two dead bodies this week might draw attention. Besides, the cacao flower he pointed out truly has beautiful skin. Flipping him the middle finger, I stalk down the length of the bar to the woman he pointed out.

When I'm less than a foot away, my tongue twists over

what to say. Usually, I flash a dimpled smile and meat stumbles over themselves to please me. Easy fucking prey. I clear my throat while leaning a little closer to let my arm brush her shoulder. She jerks wary brown eyes up to my face. My lips twitch when they widen slightly, no doubt tracking the tattoos lining my entire throat.

Wide, full lips part slightly and my eyes follow them as if spellbound.

"Hello," I whisper, then lean closer in case she can't hear me. Her body shifts minutely away, but I don't miss the spark of interest in her brown pools.

"You're pretty," I tell her and my face heats at the simple compliment. But my brain struggles to come up with something more original.

"Thank you," she breathes, racing her eyes over my face, neck and the tattoos decorating my arms. A black short-sleeve shirt allows her to see how much ink mars my skin. A pulse beats rapidly in her neck and I get the impression she likes what she sees.

"You're very pretty," I amend, unable to take my eyes off her alluring features. A husky laugh spills from her lips and my cock jerks in my pants. Warily, I take a step back. My cock has never done that in reaction to meat.

"Look," she says, her silky voice cascading over me. "You're hot, I'll give you that. But you barely look old enough to buy me a drink. So, tell whoever put you up to this that I said you're hot and gave you my number."

Ice trails down my spine at the pity layering her words. As far as rejections go, it's a polite one. And it pisses me the fuck off. Resisting a snarl, I step forward, invading her personal space. She gasps and without tearing my eyes from her, I rap my knuckles on the wooden bar top.

Prey enters my peripheral vision. I hold up two fingers, enjoying the display of her pupils expanding.

"I'll take two of what she's having," I bark out, only darting my eyes away from my flower for a moment to make sure the bartender mixes the drinks. A curt nod and quick hands fly to a glass and a clear bottle of liquor.

Training my eyes back on the wide-eyed doe in front of me, I flash my famous dimpled smile.

"I lied," I tell her, feeling the truth of the statement settle in the marrow of my bones. "You're not pretty," I sneer, silently relishing her lips dropping open in shock. They'd look damn good wrapped around a cock, but I'm not ready to stick my dick in meat just yet, not even bewitching ones.

"You're fucking radiant." A glass thuds to my right, but I ignore it in favor of spearing the temptress with my words. "Your skin would make the Goddess of night jealous. Your eyes sparkle like the brightest stars and your fucking smile rivals the sun."

I lean down until my nose brushes hers. She doesn't pull away, breath fanning my face. "You're a goddamn Goddess. And I'm old enough to do more than just buy you a drink." Pulling away, I reach around her for the two glasses, looking at the fruity cocktails with a hint of distaste. Deaton put me up to this so he'll just have to suck it up.

"I hope to see you around, oh, benevolent one," I tease the flower watching me with an interesting mixture of emotions. Maybe I stunned her. I definitely shocked my own damn self. Surprised that I meant every word. Who the fuck knew meat could be so mesmerizing?

I turn away, marching back to my cousin with my prize and a weird, full feeling low in my belly. It feels like something is stirring, waking up. It's not entirely unpleasant but damned inconvenient. I have two parents to slaughter.

Fucking meat is not on the agenda.

Two Months Later...

The tip of a knife presses against my tongue as I watch my prey struggle in their restraints with mounting boredom. Poor, dumb Todd, blonde hair plastered to his forehead, sweat dotting his brow. Tilting my head, I debate which vital organ to take first. Things get bloody when I get bored.

"Alright, Todd," I say, standing and stretching my arms overhead, knife clutched in one hand. "It's time to die. Any last requests?" My feet carry me to the slab he's strapped to. "Even those on death row get a last meal. Though I don't think we have the same dietary predilections." My lips curl into a sinister grin. I love this part.

"P-p-please don't do this." Tears sparkle in brown eyes. I want to pluck them. They'd go good in a clam chowder soup. Blinking, I try to remember what I asked. Oh, last requests. Smiling indulgently, I pat his head with my free hand.

"I wish I could say there's another way. But, alas, we all die in the end. Unfortunately for you, today is your day." I strike swiftly, a clean line across the throat, blood spilling down, soaking his collar. He gurgles, body jerking, fighting to keep him alive as his life's blood flows freely.

"It's so sad. He was such a good guy. Would anyone like to say anything?" I look around the empty room, imagining myself standing at an altar, a church filled with mourners. Sadly, no one steps forward to speak Todd's praise to God's ears. End scene.

"Well, that didn't completely cure my boredom, but I

guess I have food for the week. What do you say, Todd? Fillet à la Todd? That does sound good. I'm so glad you agree," I croon down at the dying man, holding both parts of the conversation.

Placing the knife down, I pull my wrinkled list out of my pocket, scratching Todd Peterson off. Poor clerk didn't have any details about my birth parents. It was his end. He should've lied, pointing me in someone else's direction.

The next name on the list is Natalia Bell. My scribbled note, fading from extended time balled up in my pocket, says she's a social worker. I drew a little arrow connecting her name to Sarah Bell, sister. Hmm. Abduct the sister to draw the social worker out or just go for gold? Or both? I like sisters. They don't always taste the same.

Eeny, meeny, miny, mo. Natalia Bell, you are it. Let's grab a bite to eat together.

SISTERS

NATALIA

FIVE

"Please be negative. Please be negative. Please, please," I whisper while staring down at the little piece of plastic in my hand that can determine my future.

"Come on, Nat! We're going to be late," Jason shouts from the opposite side of the bathroom door. Irritation flares and I try to squash it down. This isn't his fault. It's mine.

"I'll be out in a minute! My hair isn't done yet," I lie. Cool tile kisses my butt as I rest against the base of the bathtub in my two bedroom townhome. Two bedrooms because the second room is an office, not because I'm planning for a kid at forty-five years young.

Especially not with Jason.

I shove that voice aside, too. It sounds eerily similar to my younger sister, Sarah. The last time we hung out at Louie's bar, she felt the need to question why I'm still involved with a guy after five years with no ring and still living in separate houses.

Unlike Sarah, I'm not on a mission to do everything

without a man, like IVF or adoption—not that I don't absolutely adore my niece, Lauren—but some things are better with a man around, even if I'm not planning to pop any kids of my own out yet.

Or ever. Who has kids in their forties?

"Babe—"

"I'll be out in a minute, Jason!" I snap, nearly throwing the pregnancy test down in agitation.

Be careful who you have kids with.

God. I press a palm into one of my eyes. Now, that voice sounded like my adoptive mother, who disapproved of every guy I brought home in my twenties. Not that she wasn't wrong. If there was an award for having the most shitty boyfriends, I'd probably be runner up.

"I'll wait for you in the car," Jason yells, feet pounding away from the door in tune with the pulse throbbing in my head.

Okay, he's not perfect, but he's better than all the other guys I dated. And he's not up my ass all of the time. Sometimes I get consumed with work and become unreachable or distant until I've closed a case out. Jason never seemed to mind. Sarah's narrowed green eyes and dark brow cocked flashes in my mind.

Oh, fuck off, sis. At least one of us has gotten laid this month. Come to think of it, I should call her when we get back from the restaurant. She's bailed one too many times on my invitations to hangout and my big sister radar is flashing signs that trouble is a foot.

Maybe she finally got laid. Right. Dr. Bell finally unwinding, lowering her standards for a guy that doesn't have a PhD and getting railed. I can't even picture it, not that I want to imagine my sweet sister pinned under anyone.

Slowly, a single line appears on the stick and I whoop for joy, jumping to my feet, anxiously checking to make sure a second one doesn't appear. Oh, thank God. No more unprotected sex, I promise.

I'm too old for this shit. Unlike Sarah, who's tried multiple times to conceive, I've been quite content with not getting knocked up and toyed with the idea of getting my tubes tied. Menopause will render that redundant so I've put it off.

Either Jason will start wrapping it up or I'm making that appointment. It just felt so final. After tossing the negative pregnancy test in a waste bucket, I walk toward the sink to wash my hands.

You need to be more like Sarah.

Shaking my head as I towel my hands off, I try to exorcize my mother's voice from my mind. What should've been friendly competitions between sisters was fanned into all out sibling rivalry that nearly destroyed any chance of Sarah and I being close enough to consider each other friends. That was then. Our parents are dead, Sarah's a doctor, and I have a job I love as a social worker.

Walking out of the bathroom and ignoring the pang of loneliness that stirs behind my ribs upon noting Jason truly stuck to his word to wait outside, I pad over to my closet. My hands reach blindly in for the first article of clothing. After five years, Jason stopped complimenting my appearance and I stopped trying to impress him.

My hands smooth down imaginary wrinkles in the backless dress I slip on and I wonder not for the first time, *what is my life missing?*

I'm not Sarah. Kids aren't missing. But maybe someone willing to patiently wait inside the house for me while I get dressed or doesn't yell through the doors to rush the process. Coily hair like mine takes time to wrangle into something society deems "appropriate". If only Jason understood that.

I blame the hormones for my morose mood and slip on some heels. If Sarah was here, she'd probably tell me all about my luteal and menstrual phases. She lives for the gynecology shit and I enjoy her ramblings sometimes. It's soothing to have another woman that knows more about what's going on in my body than I do.

God, I miss her. I make my way out of the bedroom after giving my hair a final once over and make a strict mental note to call my sister. It's been two months since we hung out. What possibly could have happened in that amount of time that I don't know about? Dr. Bell lives on routine. If something out of the ordinary happened to my sister, I'd know about it.

SARAH

Muscles flex and I bite my lip, resisting the urge to rub my thighs together. Oblivious to my ogling, a shirtless Zaiden runs a loving hand down Sheba's scales, cooing softly at the reptile. My nipples tighten at the gentle whisper carrying across the room. My hormones are running a little haywire and I'm quickly approaching the point of no return.

I just haven't found the right time or the right words to tell Zaiden I'm pregnant. Maybe I make a sound or maybe a voice whispers to him because he whips his head up and zeros in on me standing in the doorway of what I've come to call his "pet room". My eyes stay focused on him or my skin will crawl from the various enclosures and insects flitting around in them.

The father of my child has a bug problem. He fucking loves them and finds the odd chirping, fluttering of wings and sliding of scales to be soothing. Sometimes, I'll lead him into this very room if I suspect he's having an episode or disassociating.

"My Sarah," he says, lips curling into a wide smile. I return it without stepping further into the room. Instead I lean against the wood door frame and crook a finger at him. He hurries to me, claiming my mouth in a possessive kiss when he reaches me. His mouth swallows my moan as he pins me against the doorframe.

My thigh rises, hooking around his waist to pull him closer. Our mouths part and heavy pants fill the space between our faces.

"Are you alright, my raven? You took the day off?" he asks, running the tip of his nose along my neck. Tingles rise across my skin, goosebumps pebbling. I don't tell him I called in sick because I had the worst case of morning sickness shortly after he left for his own check-up with Dr. Shaw.

A wry smile twists my lips. It's still unbelievable that I'm not only on a first name basis with *the* Dr. Benji Shaw, but I have his number on speed dial and he plays chess once a week in the park with Zaiden. They also walk the trails, enjoying the solitude of nature—or rather, Zaiden enjoys the various insects present—or simply catch up. He always seems more centered when he returns from his visits with Dr. Shaw. The man wields magic on Zaiden's mind.

"I wasn't feeling well," I tell him honestly, running my hands down his scarred torso. I've memorized every groove and abrasion at this point. A day doesn't go by where we're not connected at some point. His body has become as familiar to me as my own. I wouldn't change a thing, not even his struggles with his mental disorder.

He's mine, flaws and all. My tongue licks into his mouth and his groan travels straight to my core which clenches on air.

"Sarah," he growls, grip tightening around my neck. He's naturally submissive but my body tightens with expectation when he seizes control. I don't want sweet Dayton, who looks at me with complete adoration while I perform the most mundane tasks. I want Zaiden, who stares at me with ownership blazing in his eyes as his cock wrecks me.

Right now, I want to be owned. I want my body aching with reminders tomorrow of who I belong to.

"Fuck me, Zaiden. Make me feel better," I murmur against his lips. A mewl leaves me when he hefts me in his arms before slamming me back into the wall. My back complains but my legs tighten around his waist, hips grinding against the hardening cock in his pants.

"Mine," he growls and my pussy weeps in response. *Yes, I'm yours*. It's the last coherent thought I have before Zaiden marches us from the doorway of his "pet room" and walks us to our bedroom a couple of feet down the hall.

TEMPTATION

NATALIA

SIX

Metal scrapes against porcelain like nails on chalkboard. Little needles that jam into my brain causing micro-hemorrhages. Jason talks around a mouthful of steak with juices dripping to coat his lip.

My eyes focus on the glistening sheen and my fingers curl, resisting the urge to take up a napkin and wipe it off. He continues droning on obliviously about the new merger happening at his company.

He's dissatisfied with his position as a mid-level manager. His monotonous voice slips into condescending tones concerning the importance of his position and a permanent smile keeps my lips curled upward. It says "I'm listening and I sympathize with you" when really I want to jam a fork into his palm to shut him up.

I do none of these things, letting the crisp notes of his voice lull me into a semi-state of consciousness. In other words, I'm bored to fucking tears, but my smile never falters.

It's the same one I wear at conference meetings, board

meetings, and wellness checks. With my demure smile, I'm friendly and approachable, not an angry black woman that wants to turn a deaf ear to your problems, which is what everyone expects when they get a full look at the coily hair brushing my shoulders and my dark skin tone.

They immediately shelve me into the box of "unprofessional" and "difficult to work with", all without having a conversation with me. How odd that the man I share a bed with necessitates me donning my workplace persona as if I never turn it off, even in the comfort of my own home.

Movement flickers in my peripheral vision and my head shifts, eyes landing on someone I never thought I'd never see again. The young smooth talker from Louie's.

"You're fucking radiant."

Aqua eyes pierce me from a few tables away. Temptatious lips curl into a smirk. Black ink outlining bones shine on his ivory skin, soaking up the light. He lures my eyes like a moth to flame and I'm angry at the inability to look away.

"You're a goddamn Goddess."

He captures my gaze, refusing to relinquish it. A black button down dons his lithe torso. Only the bones tattooed on his fingers draw my eyes. Squirming in my seat across from my boyfriend, I remind myself I shouldn't feel anything toward the stranger.

"And I'm old enough to do more than just buy you a drink."

He's not Jason.

"Are you even listening, Nat?" the man in question demands. I blink at him, pulling my gaze from a distraction I do not need. In five years, I never stepped out on Jason or considered it. Many times I've considered just ending things, but each time, something held me back. Even now, I bite the words back and rise from my seat.

"Nat!" Jason hisses, and I ignore it.

"I'm going to the bathroom," I tell him, walking away from our table without waiting for a response. My heels sink into the plush carpet lining the restaurant that Jason picked to celebrate our five-year anniversary at. What should be a joyous occasion sends dread into my veins. My hands push open the door to the ladies' restroom and I wonder once more what's wrong with me?

On paper, he's perfect. Stable job, owns his own car and house. He's not eager to have kids anymore than I am. He's respectful toward Sarah whenever they're in the same room. And I haven't caught him cheating. But a small kernel inside me wishes I did just to have a genuine reason to call it quits, other than the spark fizzled out. I'm no longer sure it ever existed.

Blue eyes pop into my mind, and I try my damnedest to push them away. A stranger at least ten years younger than me, if not more, caused more butterflies to erupt in my stomach in ten minutes than Jason ever did in five years. It's a problem and the urge to call my sister sinks into me. Sarah loves solving problems and fixing people. I enjoy running from them.

The bathroom door swinging open forces me out of my spiraling thoughts. In a detached manner, I turn from the mirror that I forgot I walked to stand in front of to greet the newcomer. Instinctively, I want to make a good first impression to dispel any stereotypes attached to my skin.

Those devil eyes freeze me in place. He runs them languidly down my body like a physical touch and I resist walking toward him to feel his hands on me.

"This is the women's room," I remind him, voice pushing past a dry throat. His smirk widens, fingers turning the lock and I take a wary step back, heels wobbling with my unsteady gait.

"I know," he says. A shudder runs through me at his

smooth voice. The memory of his lips being inches from mine as honeyed words drip from them shoots through me. Shaking my head, I step further away from him. Two words. Jail bait. Or is it one? He has to be barely fucking legal, prowling closer.

"I just wanted to get a closer look without having to peer around Mr. Corporate. He doesn't seem your type," the stranger taunts.

"You don't know my type," I snap back, hackles raising. "In fact, you don't know me." My eyes dart around him toward the door, mentally calculating the distance and if I could make it in my heels. Blonde hair invades my vision, walking toward me in a circular pattern. He stops when my back faces the mirror and his faces the stalls. The door lies to my right now. An easy sprint, if I so choose.

His head jerks in the door's direction. "You can leave at any time, Goddess. I just wanted a closer look." His low timbre loosens some of the tension accumulated from sitting across from Jason. I hate it.

My chin lifts, a small sneer twisting my lips. "I don't need your permission to leave. You're the who's where he doesn't belong. And my *boyfriend* is none of your business." Quick as lightning, an unnamed emotion flashes in his eyes. There then gone like a vapor of smoke.

Long legs eliminate the distance and a squeak leaves me when his chest brushes my breast. Pale lashes lower, shielding some of the intensity in the azure pools.

"Has he told you how delicious you look tonight?" My heart races at his words, lips drifting apart on a quick intake of air. "Your skin can tempt a sinner to sin again, and again. You look glorious tonight." Calloused fingers trail a featherlight touch down my arm, but heat burrows into my skin. He *burns* me.

"I hope you go back out there feeling like the Goddess

you are and demands he worship you." Lips brush my cheek, breath fanning my ear. "I certainly would if you'd let me." My lips clamp down on a moan, eyes tempted to roll back at his praise alone. What devil did he bargain with for the gift of his tongue? Oh, I do not need to think about the things his tongue could do to me!

DALTON

Dark pupils expand, eating up some of the brown. Lush lips remain parted and full breasts heave with quick breaths.

I have no idea what the fuck possessed me to follow her into the bathroom. But her gaze from across the restaurant arrowed straight into my cock. When I saw her get up, practically running from me, my instincts took over. They demanded I chase her down, corner her, and see what the hellcat is capable of.

My fingers don't twitch for the blades resting in my pockets. No, they curl into my palm. Temptation begs me to slide a finger along her soft skin again. She is a fucking Goddess of temptation and it leaves my senses scrambling.

I've never reacted to meat this way. Maybe instead of following her and jack face into the restaurant, I should've waited on my bike a few doors down from her home and snuck in while she slept.

But after giving up on following her sister and scar face around for a week, I decided a direct approach may be best since Ms. Bell hadn't visited her sister during that time frame. When I arrived at her address and saw her sashaying out of the door, skin soaking up the moonlight, all thought fled.

All I could think was *it's her*! The fucking temptress from Louie's bar a couple of months back when Deaton once again tried to entice me into fucking an animal. And nearly succeeded.

Her scent drifts from her skin, inches from my mouth. I want a taste. It's not a craving for filleted flesh that drives my tongue to swipe across my lips. I step away from her, shaking my head of the fumes or fucking pheromones she's releasing that's rewiring my neurons.

Meat. Animal. Slice, dice, and discard. That's always been my way since Deaton placed a knife in my hand, giving me an outlet for the dark cravings banging around in my head.

"You should go," I rasp, sliding my eyes away from her. "We wouldn't want Mr. Corporate to pop a blood vessel wondering what's taking you so long. He doesn't look like the sort to come hunt you down." A healthy dose of venom layer my words and her flinching in my peripheral drive my eyes back to her.

Barely veiled disappointment gleam in her eyes and I whisper, "fuck it," before closing the distance between us and claiming her mouth in an inexperienced, sloppy kiss. Her moan wraps around my cock and tugs, forcing blood to rush to the unused organ, and hardening the flesh.

My hands pull her soft body into me. Her arms wrap around my neck, and nails scrape my scalp, sending a shudder through me. My balls tighten painfully and the embarrassing thought of spilling in my pants forces me to pull away some.

Her gasp fans my lips and I dive back in, slower. Her

tongue wraps around mine and I follow her lead, letting her teach me how to kiss her properly. My fingers knead her ample ass and my hips jerk back and forth in micro thrusts, imitating what I want to do to her.

Fucking Deaton. This woman will be my undoing and it's all his fucking fault for pointing her out to me, ripping away the barrier that divides me from seeing people as anything other than meat.

Starved for more, I pull my mouth away and close my eyes. If I don't wrangle my body under control, I'll fuck her on the bathroom counter and slit her boyfriend's throat for daring to interrupt. Messy, messy. That's what that would be and I can already hear the lecture from Deaton.

"I shouldn't have done that," she whispers, arms still looped around my neck and breathing heavy. My molars grind against each other. I only need to take her and pry information about my birth parents from her, but the temptation to put pieces of her boyfriend in my fridge is overwhelming.

But her words are the douse of reality I need, cooling the desire burning through my veins. I regret fucking nothing. But I enjoy the thrill of hunting. If my little flower wishes to run back into the arms of Mr. Wrong, then I'll let her, just so I can snatch her up later.

And he has an appointment with my blades. Oh yes, he does. His fate sealed when I saw his hands land on *my* temptress.

"Of course, sweet flower," I tell her, letting my hands slide from her ass. Damn, I miss squeezing it already. After unwinding her arms from my neck, she steps back, avoiding my eyes as she adjusts her dress. Her fingers swipe across kiss-swollen lips and pure fucking male pride sweeps through me. I did that.

"See you, around," I say with a dimpled smirk. She flinches but nods, skirting around me to prowl toward the door. I watch the sway of her ass until the door closes behind her.

Oh, sweetheart, the chase is on. And I *always* win.

MIDNIGHT SNACK

DALTON

SEVEN

Why do they always fucking squeal? I swear pigs are my least favorite animal, right next to sheep.

Another piece of meat swings from a hook in the basement of Rhys' cabin. Deaton chills with his feet kicked up on a table housing empty bottles of beer. Rhys quietly cleans his rifle, acting oblivious to the animal noises erupting from the mouth of my current prey.

Something's wrong.

Something changed, breaking off and rattling around inside me after the kiss with Natalia in the bathroom of Boudreaux's restaurant. I can't get the feel of her lips, the softness of her skin, and the buoyancy of her ass out of my head.

Dissatisfaction weighs heavily in my gut. Burying my blades in the swinging meat sack over and over doesn't dull the roar of *something* in my veins. I need to see her again.

For research. For my parents. Nodding, I swipe the back of a hand across my brow, smearing blood. Huh. I guess I blanked out again. I can't remember when the piggy stopped squealing.

"I'm going out," I announce, turning away from the strung up carcass.

"Zachary—" Deaton starts, stopping when I whirl on him with wild eyes, blood staining my skin and hair.

"Relax, *Dad*. I'm not going hunting for something else to kill. I'm going to see a flower about a lead on my parents." The lie slips off my tongue with ease and Deaton cocks a dark brow. He clearly doesn't believe me, but what the fuck ever. I'm a grown ass man. My babysitting days are over.

"Let him go, D. You won't reason with him with that look in his eye. And I'd like to not have to bury another family member so soon," Rhys replies dryly, never looking up from the disassembled weapon.

Scowling, I flip him a middle finger he ignores because I'm not sure who he thinks he'll end up burying, me or Deaton.

"Wash the blood off and don't do something stupid." Deaton's voice slips into his usual indifferent tone. Not that I needed his permission anyway, but I give him a nod before striding toward the stairs. They can clean up the mess for once.

I need to see my little temptress again. Maybe even test out if she tastes as sweet as I remember or if novelty heightened everything.

*T*wo days and she's still just as pretty. I trail a phantom finger along the curve of one cheek. Maybe she's prettier asleep.

Oblivious, eyes closed. She can't look at me with a mixture of lust and regret, like when our lips parted in the bathroom. I didn't need to ask if she regretted the kiss.

Witnessing her remorse caused an odd feeling to take up space in my chest. I have no name for it. But at least the spot next to her in the bed is empty. With the way I'm feeling tonight, I'd go against Deaton's directive to not do anything stupid and murder the man lying next to my temptress.

Fuck. Why *her*? Because she laughed at me? Or because she didn't pull away when I tried genuinely flirting with another human being, abandoning pretenses and lowering my defenses a little?

Maybe that was it. For the space of a few seconds, I allowed myself to be vulnerable, and she ate it the fuck up. And later, she didn't push me away when I kissed her, despite fumbling with the act initially. No, her regret happened after she let me kiss her.

Now, I need another taste. My eyes slide from her face to the blankets tangled around her legs. There's something else I've never done that I suddenly hunger to experience.

Natalia gifted me with my first kiss. I think it is only fair that she lets me sample a woman's flavor for the first time, too. My hands move without command, gently sliding the blankets away from her mocha legs. Damn, she has nice legs.

I can't think of a single fucking thing I don't like about her. Maybe next time, I'll talk with her longer to see if I enjoy her personality as much as her beauty.

No. Get a grip, Zac. She's a means to an end. I try to

envision the look on her face when she realizes what Samantha knew all along.

I'm a fucking monster.

But I don't let that reminder stop me from sliding her panties down her legs. Furrowing my brow, I cock my head at the white piece of paper taped to the center of her underwear.

What the fuck is that?

After sliding a finger down the center, I bring it up to the weak moonlight streaming through the window. Red paints my finger.

Fuck, she's bleeding. This really couldn't get any better. My eyes laser in on the dark curls and the puffy lips beneath them. Licking my lips, I yank her panties the rest of the way down her legs, tossing them to the bedroom floor.

I don't want to taste her from a fucking napkin. I want to drink straight from the source, like my own personal tapped keg.

Yes, little flower, give me all of your nectar. Settling on the bed without jostling her is tricky and I frequently dart my eyes to her face to ensure I haven't woken her up. If I do this right, she'll chalk this up to a wet dream, and I'd have satisfied an odd craving of mine. We both win.

Lying flat on my stomach between her legs, I don't move hers aside. No, I focus on her opening and the bit of blood sticking to her lips. Using my fingers to part her folds, I drive my face forward, groaning when she coats my tongue.

She tastes so fucking good. The blood mingles with her naturally sharp taste. It's an odd cocktail, but the metallic taste of blood is familiar. I wonder if I can make her taste even sweeter next time. I'll have to look that one up, but for now, I swipe my tongue in and out of her channel, letting her blood flow to land on my tongue.

Weak moans spill from her and I switch from gluttoning myself on her flavor to trying to tease more moans from her. Her hips move slightly, encouraging me. My free hand snakes down, sliding into the waistband of my pants and stroking my cock.

It's only ever risen for her. She's truly a fucking enchantress, weaving a spell on me. But fuck it. If she wants me to be her damn slave, I'll do it so long as she lets me eat her up anytime I want.

My tongue mimics my hand, sliding up and down in tune with my rough strokes. Her moans get louder and her hips lift more and more off the bed. She's close and I want us to detonate at the same fucking time.

Come for me, sweet flower. Let me taste it.

I say none of that. When her hips jerk as I slide my tongue around a little nub above her slit, I switch tactics again. Clearly, it's a pleasurable spot for her. I wrap my lips around it and suck at the same time I jerk hard on my cock.

"Ah!" she moans, whimpers chasing the sound. I keep sucking and swirling my tongue until pleasure zips down my spine and my cock twitches, releasing in my pants. Panting against her pussy, I rest my forehead on her mound.

Shit. That was better than any fantasy I could've cooked up in my head. Risking a glance up, I notice her lashes still rest on her cheeks, but a delectable flush stains her skin. I guess it was as good for me as it was for her. It's definitely going on my list of things to do again.

I'm in so much fucking trouble when it comes to Natalia Bell, but I can't bring myself to care as I slowly extricate myself from between her lush thighs. Sliding off the bed, I smirk at the wet spot right between her legs. Blood isn't the only thing that leaked onto those sheets.

I don't wipe the liquid coating my chin. I want to leave her home while wearing her on my face. Kneeling down, I pocket the discarded panties and pull the blankets back over her. If she can sleep through that, then I'm sure her mind can come up with an excuse for why she went to bed without underwear.

Affording myself one final glance at her sleeping form, I creep out of her bedroom.

A week. I'll give myself a week to clear my head, plan for housing my alluring guest, then I'll snatch her up like I did her panties.

A week. Surely, I can get whatever the fuck she did to me out of my system in a week, right?

Of course, I can. I've never let prey get the best of me before. Even if I am still wearing her blood and juices on my face.

I'm the hunter and she's the meat. That's all there is to it.

But I can't shake the fucking feeling that I'm lying to myself.

THE OTHER WOMAN

DALTON

EIGHT

How. Fucking. Boring. My fingers twitch around the blade that made its way into my hand. Dark lashes rest against mocha skin, full lips parted, letting out huffing breaths every few minutes. A black cap hides dark hair the same shade as her furrowed eyebrows. She's asleep with her forehead creased and I shoot a glare at the waste of flesh sleeping next to her.

I can kill him. The knife begs me to feed it life's blood, staining the pretty metal a lovely shade of red, but that's messy. I need to take Natalia and do it in a way that doesn't raise alarm because who the fuck knows how long it'll take for her to break. After the run-in at the restaurant and my snack a couple of days later, I thought staying away for another week would dull the effect she has on me but the urge to kill the man sleeping next to her presses insistently against my thread of self-control.

He's a waste of flesh that doesn't deserve my temptress. Stepping carefully along the plush carpet in the spacious bedroom, I make my way to Mr. Wrong's side of the bed.

His phone charges on the nightstand and inspiration sparks.

Snatching it up in a gloved hand, I kneel, sliding a finger up and tilting the camera to capture his face. It unlocks. Hello, Cami, why are you texting Natalia's man at —a quick glance at the time—three in the morning?

> I miss you.

> > I can't come over tonight. Nat will suspect something. I stay over every Thursday night. And last week was our anniversary.

My throat urges my mouth to gag, and I'd vomit if I could. Dull face, you're barely attractive enough to pull the Goddess sleeping next to you. How the hell did you pull a —my eyes squint at the small icon for Cami's contact photo—woman at least ten years younger than you? Meat rarely makes sense. But I've stumbled onto this drama and it's definitely more entertaining than watching the unhappy couple sleep.

> When are you going to tell her? I can't keep waiting. Ditch the old bitch.

Glaring at the screen, I click her photo. Full name is Camilla Boston. Count your fucking days, Camilla aka Goldilocks, who should've gotten eaten for sleeping in the wrong fucking beds. Well, you crept into the wrong one and I like nothing more than righting wrongs. Another glance into the incriminating messages reveals another noodle of information.

> Jason, you know I love you.

Jason dies too. End of story. Tomorrow, I'll take Natalia and free up some damn oxygen on this planet by removing the flesh from meals one and two. Placing the phone back on the nightstand without reinserting the charger, because fuck you Jason, I creep out of the bedroom, closing the door quietly behind me. Good thing they don't have kids. That could get real messy.

I sneak out the way I came, through the backdoor. Swiping Natalia's keys earlier in the week and making copies proved ingenious. No broken glass or signs of forced entry. No, officer, I was never here. Though the idea of slicing Jason's carotid with a piece of glass sounds fun.

A booming bark from the neighbor's dog momentarily paralyzes me. My head swivels to lock eyes with the big fucker. Saliva drips from bared teeth and I growl back. Game on. Let's rumble.

NATALIA

Waking up alone shouldn't be a relief from one half of a couple who's been together for five years. But a relaxed breath eases out of me upon spotting the empty place next to me that Jason slept in the night before. Sitting up and swinging my legs off the bed, I bask in the security of not being pregnant once again, which would tighten the noose that is Jason around my neck.

Maybe my hormones needed a jumpstart like an illicit kiss with a stranger in a bathroom, because my cycle started that night shortly after arriving home. It also provided me with the perfect excuse to not sleep with

Jason while I still felt the ghost of John Doe's lips on mine. I should've asked for his name, but I think kissing a guy behind my boyfriend's back is borrowing enough trouble.

A name leads to a phone number, and that leads to me cheating instead of breaking things off with a clear conscience.

Today will be the day.

With that decided, I quickly get dressed for work, losing myself in the process of untangling and moisturizing my hair after padding to the bathroom. When my curls fall in a thick, coily arrangement around my shoulders, I walk out of the bathroom, snatch up my phone and hurry down the stairs. My lips curl into a scowl when I spot a text from Jason.

I had an early meeting at work this morning. Call you on my break.

My eyes roll and I leave him on read as I rush out of the front door. I'm sure he has plenty of ass kissing to do before the merger goes through. Leaving thoughts of Jason's less than masculine qualities at times, I hop into my car and drive to BJ's Coffee.

When I pull into the parking lot, I can barely hold in a growled, "fuck." At a little past eight, there's still at least ten cars parked outside the cozy, family-owned coffee shop. Getting out of the car, I hurry toward the frosted glass door of the front entrance.

I can't stop the happy inhale of vanilla and coffee beans. Only two patrons stand at the front counter and, without looking around, I take up a position behind them. My mind and body need caffeine, especially on the day I decide to break up with Jason. I'll have to give Sarah an abridged version over the phone until we can link up.

"Next," Jeremy calls, beaming at me when I approach.

The other two patrons walk over to the mobile orders section. It must be my lucky day.

"Hi, Jere. I'll take the usual with a ham and cheese croissant," I tell him, grimacing after the words leave my mouth when I realize I left my purse in the car. My eyes close for half a second before snapping open with a will of their own.

"Here," a familiar, deep voice says, a tattooed arm reaching past me and a muscled chest pressing into my back.

"I'll get what she's having and charge my card," the stranger that I've run into three times now says to Jeremy. The youngster darts brown eyes between the two of us before grabbing the proffered debit card. My limbs stay locked into position.

Warmth seeps into my skin from the press of our bodies. Soft lips graze my ear.

"Morning, sweet flower. Why don't we move aside so someone else can order?" he teases, his voice causing my nipples to tighten. I nod breathlessly, moving without thought to the left. More air whooshes out of me as I allow my eyes to take in the people sitting at the tables spread out through the establishment.

Sunlight kisses Jason's dark hair, making it glisten from his overuse of pomade. Across from him, a petite blonde smiles with one hand resting possessively on his arm. He doesn't shake it off, lips moving animatedly and brown eyes shining with soft affection.

Did he ever used to look at me like that?

"Natalia!" A voice shouts and my head swivels to Jeremy behind the counter with my coffee cup in hand. I reach for it with nerveless hands, ignoring the handsome stranger watching the scene unfold. By the time I turn back to face Jason, he's spotted me. Wide eyes glance from me to the man at my side.

Oh, no, you don't.

My heels click across the wooden floors and his blonde companion finally looks up to see what grabbed Jason's attention. Her red-painted lips fly open and a glimmer of fear enters her eyes. Good. Today, I might just prove the stereotypes right.

"Jason. I thought you had an early meeting. At work," I say, staring pointedly at the table and half-eaten pastries and Styrofoam coffee cups.

"We were just—" My hand raises, cutting off the blonde's useless explanation.

"I'm not talking to you. I'm talking to my boyfriend of five years," I say, training my eyes on his reddening expression as his eyes take in the curious gazes of everyone present. Silence reigns in the coffee shop I've visited religiously every week since moving five minutes down the road a year ago.

Mr. Albert, Jeremy's dad, must've cut the music off so everyone can hear Jason's explanation for why he's sitting across from a woman that isn't me after lying via text. We had our first coffee date here. Tears sting my eyes, but I don't let them fall. This was long overdue. But I somehow thought I would be the one to end it.

"Nat." Jason swallows nervously before wetting his lips. "Things haven't been good for a while," he says in a reedy voice. I nod in agreement. I'm no saint, but at least I planned to end things before hopping in someone else's bed.

Wordlessly, I flick the cap off the cup with my thumb and dump my hot coffee in his lap. He jumps up with a scream and movement flashes to my left.

"Try it, bitch, and watch me sweep the floor with you," I

snarl, stepping closer to the other woman to drive my threat home. She slowly sinks back into her seat with a fearful expression.

Satisfied with her submission, I turn on a heel and march the fuck out of the coffee shop, ignoring the open-mouthed stares following me. I'm sure someone will call an ambulance.

While walking to my car, I make a note to call my sister and ask if she knows a good lawyer in case Jason presses charges for assault. I hope his damn dick melted off.

RUN

NATALIA

NINE

"You're what?! And he's how old?" My head throbs, listening to my sweet, reasonable sister tell me how she banged a stray and got knocked up. Oh, and he's psychotic. And I thought my pregnancy scare and Jason's cheating would be the most shocking thing discussed during our conversation when I called after things settled down at work. Shockingly, Jason hasn't sent law enforcement to pick me up.

"Don't judge. I'm telling you before anybody else. I don't know how to tell him," she whispers. The *him* must be nearby. How reckless, having a kid at our age. I tell her just that, adjusting my position in my office chair, night darkening the windows. I really need to get going. Hopefully, Jason doesn't have a personality transplant and waits outside my place of work to retaliate for burning his cock with my hot coffee.

"You should've used protection and then I wouldn't judge. We're too old to be having damn kids, Sarah. Lauren will flip. Oh, wait. She's also with a psychopath." I massage my temples, letting the phone lay flat on my desk, Sarah's voice coming through the speaker.

"Xavier treats her well—"

"Before or after he kidnapped her? Before or after he made her a missing person and fugitive of the law?" I don't keep the snark out of my voice. It's hard to not adore Lauren, the perfect child, emulating Sarah as best she could. It churned my stomach. I love my sister, but our parents always sung her praises at home, for pursuing a job in healthcare, as if I don't save lives too. It would've been nice if Lauren went into a field similar to Auntie Nat. She didn't. And now her career is over thanks to Xavier Lasher, father killer.

"Were you the one who called the police? Lauren swears I called them and promised her a head start, but I meant a head start with work, covering for her when people asked questions about her whereabouts." Guilt stabs at me, but I shove the bitch away. I adore my niece too much to let her throw her life away, and now my sister is traveling the same route.

"I plead the fifth, and I say get rid of it." Silence meets my words and I momentarily fear I overstepped, but it needed to be said. Sarah is the sweet, compassionate one and I'm the bulldozer. We balance each other out. And I've had a shit day, so maybe my judgment is skewed.

"I'm going to pretend you didn't say that. Goodnight, Nat." The line goes dead and guilt returns vengefully with little knives, stabbing in quick succession. I fucked up. I'm on a roll today. Sarah adores children, delivering them for a living, for fuck's sake. My head sinks into my hands. I don't know how to come back from that one.

A door creaks down the hall, jerking my head upright. The fuck? No one but me should be in the office. My hands swipe my phone, snatch up my purse and jacket, feet scurrying toward the door. I need to get the fuck out of here before trouble shows up. My niece and sister were both ladynapped. I'm not risking it.

Easing the door open a crack, I peer out into the empty hall, a relieved breath whistling between my teeth. Thank God for small miracles. I step into the hall, closing the wooden door behind me. Glancing frequently over my shoulder, I hurry to the front door; the distance closing. Right before I reach it, a figure steps from the shadows, sending fear skittering down my spine. Oh, fuck no.

"Look. If you want money, I'll give you all of it. But, please let me go. I won't even report this to the police," I bargain, taking a wary step back, heart in my throat. An evil laugh rips from the shadowed figure. My eyes bug when he utters one word, "run." I drop everything, turning tail, forgetting he's in front of the only exit.

DALTON

Like a sweet little morsel of food, she turns and obeys, feet slapping against the linoleum floors. I laugh, letting it boom free, echoing off the walls. I like it when prey runs scared, even if Natalia is altering my opinion about her particular meat. My cock hardens, and not just because she's scared.

I want her, but I haven't decided what to do about it. Fucking animals is disgusting, a depraved act reserved for mindless beasts, of which I am not. At least that's what I tell myself, but every time I see her, I question my stance. I let her run a foot or two, strolling forward to collect her things from the floor. When I've given her enough rope to hang herself, I sprint after her. It's dinnertime, babe.

She pulls on a doorknob every few feet, delicious sobs spilling into the air. I want to swallow it up. Every. Last. Drop. She collapses near door number five. Not a lucky number for her, I'm afraid. My lips form a smile she can't see. I coated the doorknobs in a paralytic toxin and she touched five of them, absorbing it through her skin. This is why we wear gloves, children.

Whistling a tune, I slow my sprint to a jog to a sedate walk. Nary a care here folks, squatting down to get a good look at my prey as if I hadn't seen her just this morning. Mocha skin, hidden behind layers of clothing, causes my mouth to water. I'll have to cut the clothing away before I strap her down for questioning back home. I'm real broken up about that, having to expose more of her delicious skin. Black curls coiled into tight ringlets frame her slack face.

"Poor wittle flower. Today is not your day. Heartache got you down?" My smile is all teeth, having had a front-row seat to her very public breakup that morning in the coffee shop. After scalding her ex's dick with her coffee, sweet Natalia went to work right after, like business as usual, but sorrow lurks in cocoa eyes. Mhm. Hot chocolate sounds nice. I wonder if she'll taste as sweet.

"Don't you worry," I bop her nose with a finger, grimacing when it brings up memories of my adopted mother. Her meat had been tough. "I'll eat you, I mean clean you right up." Not wasting the moment, I scoop her up into my arms, resuming my whistling.

She worked late. The video cut off just as she exited her office. No one will question when she doesn't come into work tomorrow. Her body conforms to mine, all supple curves, raising my eyebrows—I do not fuck animals. Gritting my teeth when my cock twitches, I decide the temptress may have to die sooner rather than later.

As soon as she tells me everything about my birth parents, starting with the fucker who spawned me.

SECRETS

SARAH

TEN

Tears sting my eyes as I end the call with Natalia. Sniffing them back, I press a hand to my closed eyes. Yes, she had a rough day, but that's no excuse for the cruelty of her words. I never judged her stance on children, but I at least expected her to be a little more supportive of mine.

"Little raven?" Dropping my hand, I whirl around to face Zaiden, who stands in the doorway of our bedroom, looking at me with a mixture of wariness and hesitant joy.

"How much did you hear?" I ask, bottom lip trembling. He slowly steps into the bedroom, broad shoulders hunching forward, as if ashamed of being caught eavesdropping. His ears turn a shade of red and his eyes dance around my face.

"Enough. Are you—" He blinks rapidly without finishing the sentence, one hand gesturing at my flat stomach. Biting my lip, I nod, with my heart climbing up my throat. This is the moment of truth.

A steady drum pounds behind my ribs as I wait for him to digest my confession and react. In the whirlwind of getting him adjusted to the normalcy of life outside of mental health facilities, setting up appointments with trustworthy psychiatrists, trying out various meds to get him regulated and meeting Zaine and Zoe, we hadn't broached the subject of children despite having unprotected sex just about every other day.

It's like he poured gasoline on my libido and his cock is the match to light the fuse. With him, I'm insatiable and he's just as crazed for me in spite of the stray strands of gray hair I find every few weeks, the fine wrinkles settling into my skin and my looming appointment with menopause. This pregnancy had made me question what the hell am I doing with someone as young as Zaiden?

But my mouth won't open to express my doubts and insecurities. Fortunately, I don't need to. His long legs eliminate the distance between us and he pulls me roughly into his arms, burying his face against my neck.

"Is it really true? You're having my child?" I nod as I wrap my arms around him, inhaling deeply. Some of my anxiety settles at the choked emotion in his voice. He doesn't sound upset or disgusted. I can't believe I even wondered that he would.

His shoulders sag and the arms wrapped around me tremble slightly. My fingers skate up and down his nape and the fine hairs resting there.

"We're going to have a baby," I whisper into the ear near my lips. A shudder travels through his large frame, his grip tightening around me. I pull away and tug on his hair. His mouth claims mine immediately, teeth nipping my lip, a quiet admonishment for keeping our baby a secret from him. Hands travel down my back to grip my ass and press me into the erection straining Zaiden's pants.

Our mouths drift apart, and our breaths mingle.

"You should've told me," he growls softly, fingers

kneading my flesh. I nod, desire and guilt clogging my throat in an odd mixture.

"No more secrets, Sarah." His nose slides along my cheek. "Do you think I should punish you for keeping this from me?" Holy shit, my thighs clench tight and I fight a moan.

Zaiden had NEVER done that, but suddenly, I want him to. I'm enjoying this side of him entirely too much. Call it pregnancy brain, but lately I've been eager for him to take the reins. Like settling into a new skin, he's eased into it, growing more confident and playing my body like an instrument that he's mastered. It's easy to forget he was a virgin when we met. Or more accurately, when he kidnapped me after stalking me.

Suddenly, one of his hands flies up to my throat, quieting my wandering thoughts. My attention hones in on the male in front of me. Gently, he applies pressure, guiding me down until I'm kneeling, staring at the imprint of his cock.

Saliva floods my mouth. Zaiden's other scarred hand tugs on the drawstring of his sweats, pulling down to free his cock. Slick dampens my panties. My tongue swipes out, eager for a taste of the man that's stolen my heart and given me the one thing I thought I'd never have, a child of my own. I adore Lauren and being a mother, but some things I yearn for, like experiencing pregnancy first hand, the ups and the downs.

"Should I make you pleasure me, my raven, and leave you unfulfilled as a lesson?" he asks, eyes hooded. I whimper, leaning up, throat pressing into his hand.

"No," I whisper, watching his hand lazily stroke his hard cock. I want it.

"Do you promise to not keep things like this from me? Even if you think it'll upset me?" he coaxes. His thumb swipes a bead of pre-cum and brings it to my lips. They part easily, tongue sliding along his calloused digit. I moan around his finger. I need him inside me. Now.

"Zaiden, please. I promise. Just fuck me." My voice takes on a whiny note, but I can't help it. With him, I can be like this. Not Mom, not Dr. Bell. Just a woman in need of her man's cock.

His fingers tighten around my throat and I let out a choked gasp of surprise.

"I've never hit you, Sarah. But the next time I will spank you. Would you like that?" Oh, fuck. Where did this side of him come from and why did it take so long to unearth it? Maybe hints of it were present before but never like this. My clit throbs for him.

"Yes," I answer honestly. "Do whatever you want with me, Dayton. I'm yours." His eyes close like my words struck a nerve before snapping open. Fire blazes in glacial depths.

"Get on the bed. Face down, ass up. If I go too far—"

"You won't. I trust you," I reassure him, my hands coming to cup the one around my neck. He frowns, some of the heat dimming. I wonder if the voices in his head war with my words.

"You're pregnant, little bird. I don't want to hurt you. But I like playing like this," he says, thumb rubbing up and down my carotid artery.

"Zaiden—" His growl cuts me off.

"On the bed, Sarah. If you want me to stop, say 'Daniels.' Got it?" Mouth dry, I nod eagerly, strands of hair brushing my cheek.

"Good girl." His head jerks toward the bed and I don't wait for him to give the order again, jumping to my feet. I want him to fucking wreck me and forget all about my sister's words.

ZAIDEN

A man with no skin stands near the head of the bed, leering down at Sarah's prone form—hips raised off the bed like I asked—with a toothy grin. I blink once. Twice. He's still there, shooting me a wink from an eyeball that sits like an over-easy egg in his skull.

Deciding to ignore his presence, I walk toward one of the cherry wood dressers. My Sarah wishes me to punish her. Her pulse sped up against my palm when I suggested it, beating like those pink rabbits on television with a drum. Who am I to deny my raven?

Leather slides against my palm as I pull a belt free from one of the drawers she assigned to me. I've never done anything like this but instinct and a strong desire to please my Sarah guides me. My hands slip a thin camisole from the drawer before I stride back to my raven. Dark lashes rest on her cheeks.

Upon hearing my approach, emerald eyes pop open to follow me to the bed. They widen when they land on the belt, but I don't provide an explanation as I climb onto the bed and loom over her stretched out body. Leaning down, my lips trail along her cheek.

"Are you sure this is what you want?" A shaky breath slips from lush lips and she nods, letting her eyes drift closed again.

"Say 'Daniels' when you want to stop," I remind her, sliding my hand down to gather up the silky shirt. She doesn't fight me as I loop the front around her eyes, craning her neck back so I can tie the back to make a rudimentary blindfold. The woman in one of those romantic films she had me watch with her appeared to enjoy being blindfolded.

Sarah's pliable, slumping back to the mattress after I obscure her sight. Shuffling down until I'm straddling her hips, my fingers slide into the crevice of her thighs and push her shorts and panties aside so I can stroke her slick folds. Already, she coats my fingers, offering soft moans as I caress her tender flesh.

My other hand snatches up the belt. Trepidation zings through me and the skinless man leers closer. Ignoring both, I pull my hand back and let the leather kiss her ivory skin. Her gasp mingles with a moan as I slide a finger into her wet channel. It grips me, pulsing around my digit. She likes this.

So I do it again, cock twitching upon receiving the same result. Her moans glide around my cock, stroking the feverish flesh. I keep it up until she cries out loudly, body jerking beneath me. Her pussy clutches my finger tightly and I keep stroking her walls and circle her clit while letting the leather belt turn her skin a pretty shade of ruby.

When her moans subside to weak whimpers, I slide my finger free and bring it to my salivating mouth. Her taste lands on my tongue, making me groan. My cock jerks impatiently, eager to slide into my raven's slick hole. She's more than ready for me.

I toss the belt to the floor and shove my sweats down until my cock can slide through her folds.

"Dayton," she moans, lifting her hips to ease my entry. We both groan when my cock eases into her soaked pussy.

"Oh, Sarah," I groan, dropping my forehead to her neck. Sweat dampens her skin. I won't last long inside her and she shifts beneath me, hungry for my cock to stroke her insides. My hips retreat and her whine urges me to slam back into her, sending our flesh slapping together.

"*Ung*," she grunts, taking my hard thrust while her walls spasm around my cock. Fuck, she likes this too. I'm a goner, pulling my hips back and repeating the action.

"Dayton!" she cries weakly and pushes her hips back. My cock twitches with the need to release, but I need to make this more than just good for her. She wanted to be punished. She doesn't get to come again, but I don't know if I can stop it. My cock slides in and out of her at a rapid pace, her moans spurring me on.

Pleasure tightens my balls and I groan on the next thrust, fitting my hips flush with her ass cheeks and emptying my seed. She moans, wiggling, milking my cum. My eyes roll slightly and I pant heavily, holding still as she slides back and forth on my softening cock until a weak orgasm causes her pussy to tighten.

"Sarah," I groan, collapsing on top of her. A muffled laugh jostles me and I slide off of her, cock slipping from her pussy with a wet sound. I land on my back next to my raven, curling a strand of hair around my finger.

"No more secrets, little bird. Promise?" I ask, tugging on her hair. She shoots me a dazed smile, eyes unfocused. Her head nods in agreement while her palm slides to snake up and down my chest.

"Promise," she reiterates. My body loosens. She promised, and she's never let me down before. Sinking into the soft mattress with her juices drying on my exposed cock, I blink lazily up at the ceiling. Life with my Sarah keeps getting better and better despite the apparitions haunting me.

And now she's carrying my child. It's more than I could have hoped for all those years ago when my mother urged me to find my brothers.

MEATING DALTON

DALTON

ELEVEN

She's beautiful. I want to carve up her face so it can't tempt me to continue testing the softness of her lips, the texture of her tongue and the sensitivity of her neck. My first kiss from her lips still haunts me. And so does the taste of her pussy. I shouldn't have gone to her that night.

Her head rests at an angle, arms strapped at her sides. Metal restraints encircle her ankles and loop around her slender neck. Pretty as a doll, all chained up.

Sighing, I give a false salute she can't see, striding from the room, engaging the deadbolt on the way out. Pulling my phone free from the back pocket of my jeans, I swipe open my tracking app. Hello, Jason. Did you order a large pepperoni pizza with a side of chloroform with an appointment for filleting later? Yes, yes, you did. You ordered it when you touched my temptress and later flaunted your infidelity with Goldie, who'll get her just desserts soon.

Taking the stairs two at a time from the sub basement, my body thrums with excitement, blood rushing through every orifice. I can't wait to spill it from every one of Jason's holes. We can play hide the pin cushion. Or is it who's the pin cushion?

Making it to the top, I swirl on a heel, slamming the door loudly. I live alone and my neighbors died from anthrax poisoning several months ago. Pity, no one has come for a wellness check up. Poor fuckers.

I hum the chorus to a song, heels striking marble flooring, body tight with the eventual thrill of a kill. No high compares, no drugs or sex can top the feeling.

Are you sure about that? The phantom feeling of plunging my cock into Natalia's tight pussy invades my body. I shake it off. I've never fucked meat. But soon, Jason will wish he hadn't touched my sweet flower's meat.

I'm sure he'll also wish there was a mountain he could hide from me behind. I can practically smell the piss wetting his pants already when he realizes he's going to die. It's going to be such a lovely thing for Natalia to wake up to. Who doesn't want to see their ex disemboweled?

Walking out the door, night air kissing my hair, I keep humming, swirling my keys around one finger. What a night.

NATALIA

My head weighs a ton, lolling to the side. Blinking my eyes open is a chore I'm considering abandoning on the fifth try. Moving my tongue around in my mouth brings tears to my eyes. Fuck, this has got to be the worst hangover. I'm so sending Jason to the store for Ibuprofen and something to wash it down with.

"Rise and shine," a voice sings songs. Who? My brows dip and my face twitches. A firm touch to one check eases a snort from me.

"Oh, you are so out of it, little bird. Come on, wake up for papa," a silky voice croons, tightening my nipples. That's definitely not Jason's voice. Wait. Didn't he choose bimbo barbie over me? And does that voice belong to John Doe?

My eyes snap open, vision blurring. A handsome face wavers above me, smiling down like I just gave him the best news of his life. Dimples in each cheek draw my eyes and those pillowy lips he's curling into a smirk. They look kissable. In fact, a vague memory of kissing them teases my mind.

"Okay, doll face, you're not waking and papa is getting bored. So, I'm going to start stabbing now, okay?" He winks, moving away. I turn my head to follow, eyes widening when they lock with Jason's terrified gaze.

"The fuck?" I think I say, but my tongue struggles with lifting.

"I can't understand you and Jason has volunteered to be tonight's entertainment, so hang on to your seat, Goddess. This is about to get good." A taut ass in jeans faces me, leaning down to snatch tape from Jason's mouth. He lets out a high-pitched scream, hurting my ears.

A hard slap echoes in the room.

"Come on, Jace. You weren't screaming like a little bitch when you were balls deep into Goldie. Don't crap out on me now." The blonde stranger I now remember kissing just last week, points a finger in Jason's face to enunciate his point. Then he jerks his hand down, holding a knife I didn't initially see, stabbing straight into Jason's thigh, eliciting another chilling scream.

The fucker throws his head back and laughs, rising to walk to a tray full of instruments. I whimper, closing my eyes on the tears swelling.

"Wait your turn, sweetheart. If you play your cards right, it'll never come," the stranger remarks. My teeth bite down on my lips, fingernails digging into my palms.

The stranger pays me no mind after that, turning his attention fully on Jason, pulling scream after scream free. Tears trail silently down my cheeks and I think my nails drew blood, but I'm too afraid to open my eyes and look.

In between screams, the blonde hums and whistles, taking enjoyment in my ex's pain. It goes on for what feels like hours.

When silence settles into the room, I open my eyes, wet with tears, looking over at Jason and wishing I hadn't. A flayed skeleton sits where Jason used to, facing me, flesh peeled off, mouth stretched open in a permanent scream, skull devoid of eyes.

I'm going to die here.

THE TASK

DALTON

TWELVE

All too soon, my fun is over. Bloody hands rest on my hips and I glare at Jason for being such a bitch and not lasting longer. I haven't even cut any meat off. The temptation to whine and stomp my foot is strong, but I haven't forgotten about my chocolate companion. Her little whimpers kept my cock hard during the entire filleting.

Pursing my lips, I tap a finger against them, debating if it's flaying or filleting. Either way, food is food. I turn to look at her. Great. She's crying again, shutting those warm brown eyes closed. Oddly, I wanted to look into them. Would they look as pretty floating in a soup? I'm not sure I want to find out, stalking toward her, admiring the lush body stretched out on my slab.

This isn't me, it's her. My appreciation for animals never extends past how beautiful their screams sound and tender their flesh tastes.

Looking down at her, eyes still squeezed shut, I decide she needs a test. Food or playmate. Other than Deaton, I've never had a playmate. Familial bonding between us consists of hunting together and him sitting back with a beer and watching me slice off thin slices of meat until I'm bored and just start cutting to hear screams tease my ears.

I need Natalia for the information about my parents, and I can torture the password from her. But I'd much rather her willing participation. Yes, for this game, I want her to *give* it to me. If she tries to run, then she seals her fate as food. I don't have all night chasing people down.

"Open those peepers, precious. I have a task for you. You pass, you live. You fail, you die. It's simple." Folding my arms, I wait for her to obey. They blink open slowly, traveling over the blood coating me. I might have chunks of Jason in my hair. Fucking limp dick Jason. Eyes widening, a thunderbolt strikes my brain.

"Do you want his dick? Because I can cut that right off for you," I offer sincerely, smiling down at her. Whimpering, she shakes her head. How disappointing.

"Fine, be boring then. Are you ready for your task? Actually, let's make it spicy. Three tasks, two strikes. Two strikes mean you fail so two out of three keeps you breathing longer. That doesn't sound so bad, does it?"

"Why?" she whimpers, tears still streaking down her face. She's much prettier when she isn't crying. Should I say that? I shake my head. Meat isn't pretty. It's to be eaten. Besides, I've already told her how radiant she looks. And I'm giving her a way out of being dumb prey to be hunted and killed. She should be more grateful. It might earn her some brownie points.

Brownies. I wonder if she knows how to bake them. What was I saying? Meat. Right, playmate or prey. Two Ps. Now I want pea soup. Dammit.

"Why am I offering you grace or why are you shackled to my work table? Either are great questions." I cock my head, eyes landing on her corkscrew curls.

Maybe that's why I find myself getting lost in pools of brown. I spent a week watching her sister and her want to be joker boyfriend come and go about their day. Whipped cream does not make cacao. Natalia was adopted, like me. Two beans in a pod. Like peas and pea soup. I'm getting hungry with all these food analogies.

"Why me?" Her full lip trembles, tears clinging to dark lashes. I bring a blood covered hand to her cheek, pressing into her soft skin. She flinches, sniffling and closing her eyes while my hand stains her skin. Brown's my favorite color now.

I trail my hand from her cheek, down her sternum, admiring the sensible black bra contrasting her skin. Lower, swirling a finger in her belly button and lower still, leaving a bloody trail to her ankle. I have the insane urge to paint her red, my second favorite color.

"You're a social worker, Ms. Bell. You worked a case some twenty-three years ago," I say idly, walking to her other side to make a return trip with my hands. She flinches at every touch, goosebumps raising along her skin. Fascinating.

"A Morgan Daniels, a woman about the age I am now, was under conservatorship and pregnant with twins." My hand stalls on her hip, rage flaring hot beneath my skin. I made Jacobson Black's death too fucking quick. I'm craving a burger. What goes well with a medium rare burger? What was I saying? Oh, my mother.

"Her guardian, the dead prick." I smile, wishing I'd kept his prick too. I could've fucked Jason with it. "Allowed her to only keep one of the children, forcing her to give the other up for adoption." I waggle my eyebrows, my hand resuming its path to just below her left breast. "I think you know where this tale is going and what I'm after."

Her head shakes and I can already hear the plea on her lips. That's disappointing.

"Please, just let me go. I don't have my work computer —" My laugh breaks off the usual bleating of the weak and dying. Disappointment curls tighter in my stomach. Why do I want her to be different?

Shaking my fingers at her, I stalk away, kneeling near Jason's filleted corpse. It has a nicer ring than flayed. My hands wrap around Ms. Bell's bag, reaching in for her laptop. I turn with a victorious grin, gesturing it to her.

"I've got this. So, yes, you can give me what I want. The question is," my head tilts, eyes roaming up and down her barely clothed form. "Are you going to give it to me or will I have to cut it out of you? But we can save the fun for later. Let's get back on task."

My smile widens, incredibly pleased with myself. In my hands, rests the machine that can answer the unknown and I have a lovely catch tied down, sorrowful eyes dripping tears. A nice nut could finish the day off, but I need a new skull to fuck. My eyes flick to Jason, an idea spawning.

"What do you say, Natalia? Meat or play?" I turn back to her, cocking a brow.

She sniffles before nodding, asking, "What do you want me to do?" I crow victoriously, skipping to her, laying the laptop on a surgical trap and fishing a key from my pants.

"Ta-da." I wave it at her before approaching her shackles, unlocking them one by one. She continues lying there, eyeing me warily. Now, that's the real test. Will she run? And what will I do when I catch my little cacao flower?

I should run to a florist and see if I can purchase one. A little reminder of our time together. Slowly, she sits up, swinging her legs to dangle off the slab.

"You will clean," I declare, marching to stand in front of her. She flinches back. Scowling, I reach for her wrist, making a point. She lets me, avoiding my eyes. I pull on her wrist, forcing her to shift forward, chest brushing against mine. That's better. No running, even within the confined space.

"Clean up this bloody mess to my satisfaction and you pass task one." My head jerks to a corner of the lab. "There's a vat of acid. Throw Jason in it. His meat looks unappealing." Forcing my fingers to uncurl from her thin wrist, I step back, smile still in place.

Bowing dramatically, I plan my next move. I swipe up the laptop and walk to the door.

"I'll be back, little flower. Have this place spot less or else." I shoot her a wink over my shoulder before exiting, locking the door behind me.

I whistle on the way up the stairs from my playroom, tracing the city map in my head. Goldie needs a visit from papa bear.

NATALIA

He is fucking insane. I wish I knew that before I'd kissed him. Kneeling on my hands and knees, I run another pass of the sponge in my hand underneath the chair he killed Jason in. Bile twists my stomach and I avoid looking in the corner I dragged him into. Getting him into that acid is going to be a bitch.

Crazy fucker. Why me? Is there a target on the Bell women, the universe screaming at the psychos, "take them!". I'd be angry if I wasn't so damn terrified of the blonde killer. And why in God's name did he make the crazy fucker handsome? Ted Bundy wasn't enough? You just had to make two attractive serial killers.

And that devil is definitely a repeat offender. There's no way one kill would cool the maniacal flame in his eyes. A look he'd managed to suppress the three times we ran into each other before he took me. My skin itches, remembering his touch. It wants to peel off, still reeling.

I just—My hands stop, shoulders hunching, and a shudder runs through me. I just have to survive. Give him whatever he wants so I can make it out of here in one piece. Willing myself to look at Jason, I pray the psycho doesn't carry me out in pieces.

The floor gleams with only a mild pinkish tint. Getting all the blood out is an impossibility and not for the first time, I wonder if he's wanting me to fail.

He took my damn laptop. I swipe at tears drying on my cheeks. I can only hope he'll leave Sarah and Lauren alone. Maybe those crazy fuckers they're involved with will actually come in handy. I can film it for YouTube, three killers facing off. Shaking my head, I admit my sanity might be fraying a little.

The door creaks open and I jump to my feet, heart banging against my ribs. Please, don't kill me, I internally beg. He saunters in, smile in place, blue eyes brightening with satisfaction as he looks left and right. A whistle leaves his lips.

"Well done, little flower. You deserve a treat. But I'm hungry so we can move to task number two." His hands rub together, for all the world looking like a caricature villain.

I wish I knew a good shrink cause he's in dire need of one. My eyes drift down his body against my better judgment, noting he'd changed from faded denim and a plain white shirt into black jeans and a black button down. The color contrast suits his pale skin. He should've left the killing for someone else and taken up acting.

"Well, my flower?" He turns, smile dropping when he notices Jason's sprawled corpse.

"I was getting to it. He's heavy!" I explain hurriedly, fear spiking through me, sharp as nails. He shrugs, momentarily appearing unbothered. He crooks a finger at me and my heart sinks. What the fuck now?

LADIES FIRST

DALTON

THIRTEEN

Red truly is her color, blood staining nearly every inch of skin. My girl got her hands dirty, cleaning up my playroom.

My girl? The fuck? She's not mine. She's meat. End of story.

I crook my finger again impatiently, ready for this next test to begin. Let's see how she likes a medium rare burger, if she's capable of cooking one. I might have to marry her if she is. Oh no, if only I had someone to be my best man. I must've been too much for my adoptive parents to handle. They didn't adopt another kid. Or maybe it was the dead dogs turning up in the neighborhood that sent fear curdling their stomach?

Natalia walks over slowly, eyes bouncing everywhere but on me. Oddly, I liked her earlier perusal, eyes drifting up and down my body. Did she like it? Cocking my head, I wonder, do I want her to? I know I liked my hands on her and her lips pressed to mine.

"How did I do?" There's a slight waver in her voice, but

her chin lifts, showing a hint of a backbone. My lips lift into a smile. I always liked fireworks.

"Fantastic. Let's move this party upstairs. Task two is going to be delicious, if you play your cards right." My head jerks toward the exit and she approaches cautiously, reminding me of a skittish rabbit. One wrong move and they'll bolt. I don't move out of her way, wanting her body to brush me on the way out. It's almost comical, the way she leans nearly to the opposite side of the narrow doorway to avoid touching me.

I don't give her a break, walking tight on her heels after locking the bottom door of the basement after us. Her neck swivels back and forth constantly, likely not wanting me out of sight for long. Aw, I'm touched.

My smile dips with my eyes. Round ass cheeks lift and fall with each step up the stairs, mesmerizing me, saliva pooling in my mouth. Why have I never noticed a woman's ass before her?

Because they're meat.

Meat. Meat. Meat. Meat.

I want to bite one of them. I wonder if it's like a jelly filled donut, all creamy goodness inside. If I bite hard enough, will she gush for me? Fuck! Now, I'm thinking about other places she probably gushes from. Sonofabitch. She needs to die. Like yesterday.

"Hey!" My eyes snap from the roundest ass I've ever seen into exasperated brown eyes, a cute little flush staining her cheeks. I just know she tastes better than a burger, at least.

"Eyes up here, perv," she snaps and I laugh, enjoying her spirit. Good. I hated the tears anyway.

"Oh, I know where your eyes are, little flower. Watch your step. If you're too busy watching me, you'll break an ankle." Right on cue, she stumbles on the next step and I'm bouncing up two steps to wrap both arms around her, pulling her in tight to my body.

Holy fuck. She feels good. All soft curves and those plump cheeks I was admiring rest right against my cock.

"You can let me go," she squeaks, body held stiff. I wonder if she feels Junior waking up. Shaking my head, I loosen my hold, letting her regain her balance, before I do something stupid, like ask to taste her where she gushes. She scurries up the next few steps without once looking back, leaving me behind to stare after her.

If I don't kill her soon, I'm so fucked. Maybe I've been fucked since I tasted her mouth last week.

NATALIA

My body twitches, a live wire activated by the strange man's nearness. Freshly showered, he smelled like amber and pine, no hint of the gore that coated him earlier. And his cock moved against my butt, spurring me to flee up the stairs.

I've read this book before. It belonged to Lauren and Sarah. Tremors travel to my fingertips and I nearly jump out of my skin when I hear his soft footsteps behind me.

"Skittish, are you, little lamb?" His voice slides over me like velvet over butter. I prefer him covered in blood, eyes wild with madness than the smiling, dimpled man striding toward me, dressed all in black. He leans against the door frame of the second door, a mocking tilt to his lips.

"I want a bath. And clothes." My demand comes out only a little shaky, but I hold my ground, maintaining the two feet separating us. His head tilts in a considering manner, and I'm almost certain he's going to refuse. Until his lips stretch wide. Whatever comes out of his mouth, I'm certain I won't like.

"Under one condition, my sweet flower." He holds up one finger, dimples deepening with his smile. "You let me watch you dress." His arms cross over his chest, back resting against the door frame, ankles crossing. The picture of leisure.

Oh, I'll make him eat his fucking "condition." Two can play at being the devil. I saunter up to his leisurely lean, watching his pupils expand, until my toes brush the tips of his black loafers. Leaning up on my toes, lashes lowering, I smile when our faces are inches apart.

"My condition to your condition is that you can watch but not touch." I let my lips barely graze his before lowering to my heels, gasping when a large hand lands on my hip, fingers denting the skin.

"Deal," he growls, scraping his nails across my skin when he pulls his hand back. His other gestures at the stairs to our right.

"Ladies, first." He smirks, mischief dancing his eyes. I'm not a violent person but him, I wouldn't mind smothering in his sleep. Daydreaming of murder, I turn on a heel and march toward the stairs, feeling his eyes burning my skin. It would be a stroke of luck if *he* stumbled and snapped his ankle. A girl can dream.

A BATH

DALTON

FOURTEEN

What the fuck did I just agree to? Watch her naked? My eyes track her lush body, practically sashaying up my stairs. I don't want to see her naked. I see meat naked all the time.

But not *her* meat. Fuck! I need to kill her before she rewires anymore cables in my head. There's enough of those loose, sweetheart. Don't go adding water to a fucking dam. My hands trail along the wood bannister to give them something to do, fighting the urge to salivate some more over Natalia's pert ass.

Maybe I'd feel right as rain if I'd succeeded in my hunt. But Goldilocks wasn't where I expected, and there were too many witnesses. Probably should've roofied her drink anyway and carted her unconscious body out the front door, spewing some lies about being a friend of her boyfriend's. A real friend to the end. I should've taken more time with him.

My hands itch to hold the handle of a knife, but things bleed when I get bored, so I'd left my pocket knife behind. Now I need to scratch that itch, the craving rising again.

Natalia glances at me over her shoulder, standing at the top of the stairs. Why the hell does she have to be so alluring? I nearly stumble in my haste to close the distance between us until I'm towering a head above her.

"Bathroom?" she asks, the word coming out a tinge breathless.

"My bedroom." My mind operates on autopilot, saying the first thing that pops into my wheelhouse. My bedroom, where I want her spread out on my bed, legs open, pussy bared and dripping. She steps back as if sensing the direction of my dirty thoughts.

"You don't have a guest bathroom?" She frowns at me, a tendril of distrust entering her eyes. Oh, now she distrusts me? Not when she agreed to let me feast on her naked body. Visually.

Meat. Meat. Meat. Meat.

I point toward my bedroom door in answer, her eyes following until they alight on a gold and white wooden door, blending with the swirls painted into the hallway walls. She was a cunt who wanted to have me institutionalized, but my adoptive mother knew a thing or two about interior design. She did what she loved in the end, painting the walls. At least her blood did. I smile at the memory and Natalia flinches, walking in the direction I pointed.

NATALIA

His eyes raise goosebumps on my skin, marble flooring kissing the soles of my feet as I walk toward his bedroom. I wish I'd taken more self-defense classes after Lauren got taken. Us Bells sure have shitty luck. The freak strolls behind me, whistling some obnoxious tune, but I saw the gleam of madness lurking in his eyes when he smiled. He can't hide it. I've seen it in enough creeps on cases I worked alongside law enforcement. I never thought I'd get taken by one.

Pushing the door open, I step inside, blanking my face to hide my reaction. A four-poster king side bed rests against the right wall, white posts reaching for the etched ceiling. At the foot of the bed, an all black bench gleams, beckoning for me to sit. A black wood dresser sits opposite the bed, next to the door I assume leads to the bathroom.

Tasteful artwork graces the walls. Beautiful decor, but lacking personal effects.

"The bathroom is to your left." Fighting the shudder his voice sends down my spine, I nod, walking blindly toward the door, mind pinwheeling through different scenarios. If he has a window, am I willing to jump?

Grudgingly admitting he actually has a nice bathroom, I submerge myself beneath the water in the porcelain clawfoot bathtub big enough to seat three people. Closing my eyes, water whooshing in my ears, I let the blood wash away, taking my fear with it. Things could be so much worse.

I could be like Jason. Or raped. Or still chained downstairs.

He wants something from me. I just need to convince him to let me live past giving it to him. One task down, two more to go.

Rising from the water, hair cascading down my back, retaining all of the water it soaked up, I reach for the bath towel folded over the edge of the tub. His soap smells like him, amber and pine, woodsy and masculine. Scrubbing my skin until it itches, I try to convince myself I hate the smell.

When I'm cleaner than I was the day I was born, I step from the bathtub, water droplets pelting the floor as I pad to the double vanity housing the folded bath towel to dry myself with. Wrapping it around me, hair dripping water, I inhale deeply, mentally preparing myself to do battle with the devil.

He wants a show. I'll give him one that'll make him think twice about killing me.

THE SHOW

DALTON

FIFTEEN

One. Two. Three. Four. Five—

The bathroom door eases open slowly, disrupting the count of my bedroom knives. I keep a pouch of my favorites in one of my dresser drawers. They gleam in the light, begging me to use them, whispering "kill, kill, kill," but the sight of Natalia stepping out of the bathroom, towel draping her, hair glistening with water, silences the chant.

Curls bounce with each step closer she takes, weaving a spell on me. When she's within touching distance, eyes on my knives, leather pouch unfolded on top of the dresser, I reach a hand out to touch a stray curl. Hissing, I snatch my hand to my chest when she swats it away, glaring at me.

"No touching the hair," she snaps, showing more spirit than she has all evening.

"But I—"

"No! Do. Not. Touch. My. Hair," she enunciates each word carefully as if I'm a child, anger sparking in brown eyes. All the fuss over some hair? I blink, tilting my head, wondering if I should show her some scalps I've collected.

They don't complain about me touching them. A curl bounces, drawing my eye. They're just so springy, like those Slinkys I toss down the stairs as a kid.

Her finger raises, pointing at me like a weapon, chin lifted.

"I mean it. I'm not a pet." My lips break into a smile. It's cute. My little flower forgetting where she's at.

"No, you're a beautiful cacao flower. And I just want to touch one because it's so bouncy." Like a moth to flame, my eyes travel back to her hair.

She folds her arms across her chest, unimpressed, silently refusing to allow me to touch one curl. Just one! I wouldn't hurt it. Pouting, I run a finger down one of my blades. They never tell me no.

Shaking her head at me, she gestures at my treasures. "Are these your murder weapons?" Tears spring to my eyes and my chest aches from the laughter bubbling up out of me. She is so adorable! As if this is my only set. I swipe a stray tear with a finger. Her ears burn an umber red.

"Yes, sweetheart, these are a set of very many. Now," I glance at her towel meaningfully, cock twitching in my pants. "I believe we had an agreement and you're overdressed. Shirts are in that second drawer," pointing with the hand not caressing my babies, "and boxers are in the top drawer. I like the big dill ones. They'd look good on you." I lean to the side to peer at her ass and she snatches the drawer open with a huff.

I don't see the problem. Like any gracious host, I'm letting her wear my clothing, use my bathtub, and cook my food. It's a far fairer deal than Jason got or Goldie will get once I get my hands on her. She should be grateful I haven't killed her yet, letting her glide around my home like some Grecian temptress, curls bouncing all around her head like several Slinkys strung together.

She pulls out a random black shirt and matching boxers. How disappointing. I wanted her to wear the white ones with dill pickles and the words "big dill" printed on them. If this is what it's like having a pet, then no wonder I killed all the neighbors' dogs. Obnoxious little things yapping at me when I strolled in late at night, a body slung over my shoulder. They had to die. It was as simple as that.

"Now, now, sweetness. Don't forget our deal," I remind her, watching her ass sway away from me toward the bench at the foot of the bed. Tossing the clothes down, her freed hands reach for the top of the towel, slowly unraveling the tuck, spreading it out like wings.

Scowling, I debate marching over there and snatching it down. Her left arm lowers first, slow enough to test a saint and a saint, I am not. I don't remember slipping one of my darlings into my palm, but the cool handle calms me as the temptress teases me, lowering each side of the towel slowly until it collects at her feet.

Holy fuck. My balls tighten painfully, threatening an eruption in my pants right there. Toffee skin for days, flawless skin begging for my lips and fingers and cock. Drool could collect and I couldn't care less, feet pulling me forward until one hell of a dessert stands inches from my mouth.

NATALIA

Air kisses my tightened nipples, and warm breath floats across my nape. Heat wafts off him, warming the air between our bodies. I don't turn around, heart hammering in my chest, waiting to see what he'll do. Lips twitching, I bite them, holding back a smile, remembering his affronted behavior when I smacked his hand. My head isn't a petting zoo, but the fact he let me hit him without retaliating has me curious about what else he'd let me get away with.

Could I run?

No, long legs like his would catch me in no time, but slick coats my thighs, imagining him catching me. Nonononono. We do not fantasize about murderous kidnappers.

When a finger ghosting down my arm, raising goosebumps like the undead, I jerk away, tilting my face toward him, discovering it inches away. Dilated pupils send more dampness collecting between my thighs, clenching them tighter on reflex. He shouldn't look at me like that and I shouldn't like it.

You're a beautiful cacao flower. Is that what he'd called me moments before?

"I don't know your name," I whisper, hating the husky quality of my voice. I should not be responding like this to him, attractive devil be damned. He's a killer.

But do you really miss Jason? a dark voice whispers in my mind. I shove it aside. That's how women become accomplices, excusing illegal behavior.

His throat swallows before answering. "If I had friends, I'd have them call me Dalton. My parents called me Zachary, but it never felt like it was my name." Zachary? I step to the side, putting distance between us, and he scowls, prowling closer. But I know that name. I mean, it's probably a common name, but is it any more common than Bell women getting kidnapped? I think not. He's related to them. I feel it burrowing into my bones.

He's a Lasher.

CALL ME DALTON

DALTON

SIXTEEN

Natalia steps away from me again, genuine fear reflected in her eyes. I reach for her once more and she stumbles, tripping on the legs of the bench, slowing time down with her fall. I act quickly, without thinking, snagging one of her hands, sweeping her legs out from under her, and rolling my body until she falls directly on top of me.

A pained cough wheezes out of me, the hard flooring knocking the air from my lungs and Natalia stealing the rest. Fuck, that hurts.

"Oh, my God. Are you okay? Why did you do that?" Chocolate eyes peer down at me with concern, and I soak it up. Maybe she sensed my wires weren't quite right, but Samantha rarely tended to my bruised knees or scraped elbows, appearing almost uncaring when I got hurt as a child. Cunt. Maybe I should've buried her in the walls so she could witness this moment, a stranger showing more concern for me than she ever had, and Natalia was fearful of me less than a minute ago.

"It didn't hurt," I lie, grunting when I shift beneath her weight.

"Oh," she squeaks, moving to get off me, but I grasp her waist, forcing her to continue lying on top of me. It feels nice. She's not heavy. No, carting dead bodies with full on rigor mortis is heavy, grueling work at times. It's why I don't fault her for leaving Jason in a corner. I might have pieces of him in my fridge yet.

"Zachary—"

"Please, call me Dalton." She freezes, breasts resting against my rib cage. I shoot a glance down, admiring the voluptuous globes.

"My eyes are up here," she quips, but I can hear the smile in her voice, lifting my face to return it.

"I know, my flower," I whisper, face twitching. A shift, beneath sinew and bone, happens. It hits me. I want to keep her, permanently. Soft fingers lightly brush across my cheek. I lie still, not wanting to spook her, enjoying the brief return of the Natalia from before she learned my name. What was it about my name that had her looking at me like a frightened kitten? She saw me kill Jason, so it's not like she realized I'm a killer.

"Do you know your father?" Her voice is as whisper soft as mine was. A true temptress, voice lulling me into complacency. Shaking my head, I brazenly run my hands up from her hip, enjoying the little hitch in her breathing. I was right. She's incredibly soft, back arching slightly the higher I climb, grinding her bare pussy against my denim covered cock.

"Dalton," she gasps, hips shifting minutely. Oh, my flower is fighting it. Electric currents zip from her to me and back again, charging the air. My thumbs brush the sides of her breast, pulling another breathless gasp from her lips.

"I hate to assume, but I'm pretty sure I'm the only virgin in this scenario, so please," my hips jerk up, grinding my cock against her. Her moan is my reward. "Ride me, Natalia. You've got to know how."

"I shouldn't." Her fingers dig into my chest, hips sliding back and forth despite her words.

Smiling up at her, raising my hips to meet hers, I praise her. "That's it, baby. That feels good. Keep doing that. You're doing such a good job." She moans helplessly, hips picking up speed, tightening my balls. I'm going to come from a living person for the second time in my life.

My nails dig into her skin, urging her to keep grinding on me. Her head throws back, mouth open, releasing moan after moan. Pleasure races down my spine, balls drawing up. I'm so fucking close and I yearn to drive my cock deep into her pussy, emptying my cum inside of her.

Oh, fuck this. That's exactly what I'm going to do, rolling us until she's beneath me, beautiful skin flushed, nipples beaded and dampness coating her thighs. She's fucking dripping for me. *All mine.*

NATALIA

A needy whine slips from my lips and I close my eyes, ashamed at how close I let a Lasher bring me to climax. Dalton tsks at me, soft lips brushing over mine.

Popping my eyes open, I shake my head at him. "We can't." It sounds pathetic even to my ears, but less than an hour or who the fuck knows ago, he was pulling the flesh from my ex. Instinctively, I know we're approaching the point of no return. And it involves me screaming his name as I come.

Resting my hands on his chest, I give a weak push. He huffs, dropping like dead weight on top of me.

"Dalton!" I shout around giggles, which was probably his intent, sucking the tension from the room. His nose glides along my check, a ghost of a touch.

"Come on, little flower. We were both so close." Turning my head leaves our lips nearly colliding. Hunger stares at me through blue orbs.

"Dalton." His name is a breathless plea, but I don't know what I'm asking for. A predatory grin spreads over the landscape of handsome features, dimples winking. His lips find my neck, peppering kisses, making me arch into him. A hand glides up my thigh, teasing my folds.

"Dalton," I beg again. He can't do this to me. I shouldn't let him.

"Relax," he coaxes, fingers growing bolder. Pleasure coils within me and I lift my hips impatiently. A groan gets trapped against my skin, two of Dalton's fingers slipping inside of me. Biting my lip, I roll my hips again, moaning at the semi-thickness of his fingers impaling me.

"Fuck, love. You're so wet in here." His fingers curl, hitting a spot that curls my toes.

"Right there," I shout, rocking my hips, fucking his fingers. But before I can come apart, he yanks his fingers free, pulling a growl from me. He laughs, easing his weight off of me, unbuttoning his shirt. Saliva dries up in my mouth. I'm really doing this, watching each button pop free until he's pulling the halves off, abs flexing with the movement.

Standing up, he makes quick work of his jeans, kicking the discarded garment to the side, cock bobbing in the air.

My walls clench at the thickness, my pussy begging to be filled. Dalton kneels until we're eye level.

"I've never done this before, my sweet flower, so bear with me. There's no going back after this." His hair flops against his forehead as he shakes his head. He's right. Licking my lips, I run a finger along the veiny length. Dalton hisses, hips jerking toward me.

"Now," he groans. "I need inside you now." My legs spread wider in invitation. Dalton rushes forward, body caging me in.

"Here goes," he whispers, leaning to give me a chaste kiss, cock teasing my entrance. My legs wrap around his waist, hips raising to help ease him inside. We both groan at the first inch sliding in, my nails digging into his back. It's so thick and feels so good. Dragging my nails down makes Dalton arch, driving more of his cock into me until he bottoms out.

"Fuck," he chokes out, eyes closed, tendons jumping in his neck. I can feel his cock twitching inside me, fighting to not release immediately. It's kind of cute. Kissing the side of his mouth, I clench around him and he shouts, eyes snapping open and cock jerking, filling me with his cum. I laugh, emboldened at taking his first time and making him come on the first thrust.

"Damned minx," he mutters, pulling out, and before I can complain, he thrusts back in, hard, scooting me forward. His smile is malicious, and he picks a fast pace, cock hardening inside me, pelvis teasing my clit with each thrust. Within minutes, I'm moaning, walls fluttering around his cock.

"That's it. Come for me. Come all over my cock. It's fucking yours," he growls, hips diving into me rapidly, allowing me no time to breathe around the intense pleasure flooding me, edging me closer and closer to splintering apart beneath him. What the fuck am I allowing him to do?

The next thrust breaks me, ripping a scream of pure bliss, my body tightening around Dalton. He groans in my ear, never breaking pace, fucking me through my climax and into another like a damn man possessed.

"Give it to me, Natalia. All of it. I want all of you." His hand wraps around my throat, cutting off my gasps and pleasure slams into me. Dalton quits thrusting, grinding his hips into me, prolonging my orgasm and I can feel his cock filling me up. When the last aftershock fades, we lie there, his cock nestled within me, foreheads touching.

Fucking Lasher. I let a Lasher fuck me. Sarah will never believe this, or maybe she will.

PARENTS

DALTON

SEVENTEEN

With Natalia's naked body pressed against me, skin slick with sweat, I can feel her heart beating, slowing, rhythm trying to match mine. It feels nice. I never thought I'd enjoy gelatinous limbs and a limp, satisfied dick nestled within a woman's wet pussy, my cum leaking out around my cock.

Arms trembling, I slide my hand beneath my flower, rolling my body until she's on top of me. She grunts, walls spasming briefly around my cock, cheek pressed to my chest. Feeling victorious, I twirl a curl around a finger, sliding my thumb over the thick strand. The texture is so different from mine.

Her face tilts, eyes narrowing at my hand in her hair. I bark a laugh, jostling her some and tightening my grip.

"You're a prick," she says without heat, slumping back down. Humming, I nod. She's not wrong. Losing my smile, I wonder why the fuck people try to hide their flaws? My mother tried it. It didn't work out for her.

Bright smiling faces, sunshine, and large groups of people shine up at me from the pamphlets spread across the dining room table.

"You're eighteen now," Samantha's saying, voice coming at me from a long dark tunnel. My fingers brush one pamphlet, New Hope Sanctuary, printed in large letters across the top. Sanctuary. Another word for asylum.

"It's time you do something with your life, Zachary. You can't live off of us forever and these are our terms. You need help." The cunt's lips keep moving, but I quit tracking the sound, narrowing my eyes on the pulse in her neck.

What. A. Bitch.

But I've played this game before, and she always loses. I hope she feels the fucking gravel of dirt digging into her back from being pressed into a corner. Are you feeling frightened, dear Mother? Good.

Masking the rage incinerating the blood in my veins, boiling it to unprecedented portions, I turn to Charles Lewis, the fucking third. Praise the big guy that my biological parents demanded they keep my given first and middle name. Lewis. The only thing of theirs I can keep, if Samantha has her way.

Charles' dark hair rests at an angle, brushed off his forehead, pomade reflecting the light. A newspaper clutched in aged hands hides the spectacle of Samantha and me from view, intentionally, no doubt.

My life at the Lewis' would be more than a living hell it currently is if the dull guy didn't step in frequently, pulling me from Samantha's snares. Neither could claim the affectionate parent award, but at least Charles feigned caring if I lived or died, helping bandage my scrapes, occasionally reading a bedtime story and double checking his cunt wife didn't starve me. Being a standup guy saves his damn life.

"Father," the word slips out smoothly. No mums and paws in this house. "Why don't I work for you?" Charles lowers his paper,

salt and pepper brows shooting up. We both know I suck at math. He's the co-CEO of a merger and acquisition company, working with some guy named Lasher. Never paid attention to find out the first name.

"I can work my way up or at the least gain some experience. I can take a secretarial or janitorial position. You know I'm not picky." My molars grind at having to essentially beg, thanks to Samantha, even if it comes out as a calm request. The bitch dies today.

My eyes swing to Samantha's incredulous ones. She thinks he won't agree. Check fucking mate. Letting the smile spread across my face, oozing charm while menace dances in my eyes, I tell her, "If you're worried about my mental health, Mother, we can always get me evaluated by someone in human resources. I think they have a psychiatrist on payroll."

"That's not a bad idea, Zachary—"

"Charles, you can't be serious!" she shouts, waving a hand at me and the pamphlets but I'm the picture of perfection, blonde hair styled similarly to Charles, dimpled smile showing a hint of white teeth. He never saw what she clearly does and it will be her end.

"Give the boy a chance, Sam, before shipping him to a loony bin." He stands, snapping the paper into its original shape, effectively dismissing the conversation. Piercing brown eyes lance me.

"Get your ass to the office on time, bright and early Monday morning. You'll be my assistant, so I can look out for you. If anyone is going to teach you business, it'll be me." My father strides to his wife, who's still stammering about the institutes.

"Leave it be, woman. Come here. You know I won't be back until Monday." An arm pulls her into him and I nearly gag, rolling my eyes as they kiss goodbye. Pathetic.

"Try not to get rid of our son before I'm back," he mockingly whispers against her lips before briskly walking out of the room.

His suit case rests near the door, I'd heard the horn of Henry the driver blowing before we sat down for breakfast.

Samantha looks at me, undisguised disgust twisting her face. We stare each other down, my ears waiting for the telltale sound of Henry driving off with Charles in the backseat.

"This only buys you time, Zachary. You are going to one of these places for help." She jabs a finger at a random pamphlet. I shrug, a mocking smile plastered on my face. We shall see, bitch. With an aggravated huff, her heels click, legs striding away from me.

Big mistake giving me your back, Mumsie. Toodles. Swinging my legs out of the chair, kicking my shoes off onto the plush carpet—who the fuck puts carpet beneath a dining table? Roach magnet.

On silent feet, I close the distance and perhaps feeling my body heat, she whirls around, bringing that pale neck even with the serrated edge of the pocket knife I unsheathed and held up. A quick jerk of my hand and blood gushes. Her hands come up to stem the blood, legs giving out, but I know a fatal injury when I see one.

Kneeling near her ear, I make another cut, widening the first, blood staining carpet and marble flooring.

"Night, night, Samantha. But, don't you worry," I bop her nose, euphoria racing through me at hearing her death rattles. "Charles is in excellent hands. We both know he's fucking his secretary and spends every weekend with her. And who could blame him? He married you."

My smile drops, anger resurfacing, but I want her to die slowly, like she would've let me if she had her way. "He won't mourn for long or ask too many questions. He'll be free to fuck and marry his young secretary. I'll get the house and bury you in the basement. It works out for everyone. Really, you were the third wheel, so if you think about it, I'm doing it for Charles."

Laughing, I stand, grip an ankle, and drag the bitch to the basement. First thing I'll do with the trust fund I'll gain access to at twenty-one is build a playroom for occasions like this. Then, I'll hire a PI to discover who the fuck my birth parents are so they can truly regret handing me over to the Lewis'.

It's their fault, really, that Samantha is dying. My real mom would've baked me cookies. I whistle with every bump of Samantha's head down the stairs. Speakers would go nicely in a playroom too, so I can listen to music while I work. Samantha's last breath wheezes out of her on the literal last step of our journey, landing in the open floor of the basement.

I knew I should've just drugged her and dragged her down here, then we could've played all weekend. Oh well, live and learn, I say.

"Dalton?" Natalia's voice sends the past scampering back into whatever corridor it snuck from.

"You know him." It's not a question. Playing back the events that lead to putting my cock inside of Natalia, I recall she jerked away upon hearing my first name and then asked if I knew my father.

"Dalton—" My hands wrap around her neck and I roll us again, never letting my cock leave the cavern of her pussy. Pissed as I am at her withholding the information, her pussy still belongs to me.

"Start talking, sweetheart. Who is he? How did you know? Are you fucking him?" My grip tightens, hips surging forward. If she fucked my father, I'll fuck her so damn hard, her pussy will take the shape of me, forgetting any dick before me. Then I'll cut his dick off and fuck him with it as a punishment for touching my flower. No one touches my flower.

"Dalton," she chokes, slapping at my hands. I relax the hold on her throat, but don't remove my hands. She's got me fucked up if she thinks I'll share her.

Coughing and eyes watering, she turns her head away and I give her another hard thrust as punishment. A strangled moan slips from her and I do it again, reminding her who she belongs to now.

Mine. Mine. Mine. Mine.

I chant it over and over, hips slamming into her, feeling her walls clench around my cock. Removing one hand, I brace with it, speeding up until she's gasping beneath me, rising to meet every drive of my cock inside her sweet cunt. It grips me tightly as if it knows, too, who it belongs to.

"Natalia," I groan, balls tightening. "Fuck, tell me. Who is it? And don't fucking lie if you fucked him. He'll die either way."

"Dalton," she gasps, eyes rolling back. Fuck. She liked that.

"I'm going to peel the skin from his bones, just like Jason." She shakes her head, but I feel her walls flutter. Oh, you naughty girl.

"I'll cut off his dick, freeze it, then fuck him with it later. Maybe I'll do that before the skinning begins—"

"Dalton!" she screams, pussy sucking me in, forcing me to come with her.

"Fuck," I groan, closing my eyes, letting my cum splash her insides. I keep driving my spurting cock in and out of her, riding the aftershocks with her until we're both slumped against each other, breathing in sync.

"Lasher," she croaks. Lasher? The fuck face that worked with my father?

"I think your father is Zachary Lasher, but I never met him. I don't know him, so I couldn't have fucked him. Actually, before you, I thought I'd never let a Lasher fuck me." She keeps her eyes closed, but tears glisten in the corners.

Did Lashers hurt my flower? Because if I can slit Samantha's throat and she raised me, then blood-kin can get some too.

"Did they hurt you?" I ask softly, swiping a stray tear away. She's mine. If anyone is going to make her cry, it'll be me.

She snorts, shaking her pretty head. "No. Actually, my niece is involved with one and so is my sister." Her eyes peer up at me, searching. For what? Wait. Tilting my head, I think back to her sister, the dark-haired woman and the strange man with the facial scars.

"Your sister is fucking the Joker?" She laughs, body shaking beneath me. Her hands come up to wipe at her face, too.

"Yeah. Wait," her smile drops and she glares at me. "How do you know what he looks like? Did you follow my sister?" Her lips twist into a frown, nostrils flaring. Looks like big sister is surfacing, but was that a rhetorical question? Because it's obvious I did.

I shrug my shoulders, then to clarify, beating any imaginative fears swimming in her head, I say, "I didn't touch or harm her or the freak. I just watched. But it didn't look like you ever spent time over there, so I wasn't sure if you were close. So I followed you instead."

I don't admit I considered taking her sister to draw her out. It feels like a bad time.

Her little hands fly up, swatting at my chest. It's cute and I kiss her silent, sweeping my tongue into her mouth, collecting her flavor. Retreating, I murmur words I never thought would come out of my mouth.

"I'm sorry for following your sister. It won't happen again. I'm happy with the Bell I've got." My hips shift to remind her of where we're joined.

She gasped, shaking her head, eyes still closed. "What

am I going to do with you?" I grin because I can think of fun ways to kill time. And they don't involve my knives. Glancing down, I amend that to it only involves a spear and I can vouch for this one being safe to use.

"Perv," she whispers, pulling my face down to hers. Guilty as charged.

MISTAKES

NATALIA

EIGHTEEN

Feeling well and thoroughly fucked, I roll over, blindly searching for a warm body. When my hand meets cool sheets, I blink open drowsy eyes. Slowly, the events of the night—or day—before trickles into my mind.

Coffee house. Office. Jason. Dalton.

I jolt upright in a bed that definitely isn't my own. A shadow separates from the darkness of the room before light chases it away. Dalton stands near the bedside table and lamp. Normally full lips are pinched and his nostrils flare periodically.

"Dalton?" I rasp from a sleep-clogged throat.

"Sorry to wake you," he whispers, blue eyes bouncing around and avoiding mine. I scoot across the bed, holding the sheet to my naked chest.

"Talk to me. Why are you up? What's wrong?" My eyes lock on his tattooed chest, rapidly moving up and down.

"She—" He breaks off, shaking his head. Something's definitely bothering him.

"I don't know what the fuck I'm doing," he admits, looking across the room at the dresser pressed against the wall.

"I don't even know why I'm doing it. If *she* didn't want me, why the fuck would my birth parents?" His words pierce my heart, slinking through layers of armor and finding a weak spot. Oh, boy, I know that spiral all too well. Blinking painful memories away, I stretch a hand out, beckoning Dalton to rejoin me on the bed.

With tense shoulders and harsh breathing, he slumps to the bed, back facing me. I slide closer until I can rest my face against his back.

"I used to wonder why the Bells adopted me," I whisper into his skin. His head jerks right, but otherwise, he doesn't move. The one motion lets me know he's listening.

"They found out they were expecting a few months after my adoption got finalized. They could've switched to fostering until they found me a new home while waiting for Sarah to be born. Instead, they kept me. Sometimes, I used to wish they hadn't." Pain stabs into my chest, and I close my eyes.

I love my sister, but it took years for me to realize that. Because of our parents, I resented her and carried the guilt of hating someone unworthy of my animosity. She did nothing to deserve it. She was simply the standard the Bells held me to and since I wasn't their biological daughter, of course, I'd always fall short.

How long did I hate my skin, thinking maybe it'd be easier to be their child if at least my skin tone matched theirs?

They did that, not Sarah.

Calloused hands slide along the arms I wasn't aware I'd wrapped around Dalton. Maybe I'd unconsciously thought to physically push the pain away by pressing my body into his. He doesn't complain, nails digging into my skin. He holds me as tightly as I hold him.

"She used to lock me in dark closets for hours." His voice cracks on the word "dark." I don't need to ask if he developed a fear from it. "Sometimes she wouldn't feed me or command the staff to refuse to give me food. So, I'd lie in those closets, afraid, weak, and hungry." As impossible as it was, I press closer, wanting to absorb some of his pain so it could join my own.

"She hated me." Silence fills the room. Inhaling deeply, I confess to the one thing that nearly cost me my relationship with my sister.

"Mine didn't hate me. They just loved Sarah more." Dalton nods as if he understands, but as far as I'm aware, he grew up alone.

"They regretted adopting us. We weren't their flesh and blood, so we would always be a mistake, an imperfection in their eyes," he snarls, nails digging hard enough to draw blood. Tears leak down my face; scabbed wounds ripped open by his perfect summary of my life among the Bells.

A mistake. That's what Dalton and I were to our parents.

"I can't justify what you did, but I get why," I murmur softly, breath kissing his skin. Maybe if my parents did to me what his had done, I would've turned out the same.

"Maybe if mine had been abusive—" His bark of laughter, an ugly harsh sound, interrupts me.

"You think that's why I'm fucked up? Because I was abused?" he asks, venom seeping into his voice. Red caution signs flash in my mind's eye. That way lay danger, and it's clear he hasn't healed from his childhood trauma. But right now, he doesn't need a jury to judge him for his sins. He needs a fucking friend, and I bet he doesn't have any.

"I leave the psycho mumbo jumbo to my sister," I tell him honestly. Sarah did a stint in mental health during nursing school and probably after. Hell, the guy she is with has mental issues. She's far better equipped to deal with someone like Dalton than me.

But the idea of her anywhere near him, touching him, causes flares of jealousy to erupt behind my ribs.

Dalton's words act as a balm. "I'm so glad you're not your sister," he says, and I get the impression he means it. I rub my face back and forth across his back, soaking up his warmth. Dalton's choosing me and maybe that's what my childhood self needed to hear at that moment. Someone picking *me* over Sarah, even if he is a psychopathic killer.

Suddenly, he whirls around and pushes me to the bed, looming above me.

"I'm so glad it's you," he growls, leaning down to kiss me. He pulls back to whisper, "You're fucking perfection," and it's the sweetest thing he's ever said to me. Even better, I'm pretty sure he told me that before he kidnapped me. Smiling stupidly, I pull his face back down to entwine our tongues and wrap my legs around his waist.

Dalton rolls us and our mouths slip apart.

"Ride me, sweet flower. This time, I want you to claim *me*," he pants, hands guiding my hips along his length. Moaning, I grind my pussy against his cock, nipples hardening. Yes, this is what I want. My hands slip impatiently between my thighs and I rise on my knees, notching the tip of his cock at my entrance. Dalton watches me with dilated pupils, lips parted to allow rapid exhales.

Slowly, I slide down his cock, moaning at the way he fills me. His head tips back, exposing his neck. His groan strokes my ego. Who knew being a guy's first sexual experience could be so addictive and empowering? Nearly everything I do makes him groan like he's in pain. I kind of like the idea of torturing him. I bet that's something he's never let anyone do since becoming an adult.

"Fuck. That's it. Please, ride me," he begs and I do. After sinking to the base of his cock, I raise my hips back up before slamming down again. Oh! His cock strikes a spot not even Jason managed to find. I do that again, throwing my head back and giving into the pleasure. Dalton growls, hands finding my hips to speed up my movements. Oh, fuck this.

Leaning back on my hands, I unfold my legs out from under me so I can use them as leverage to fuck myself with Dalton's cock. He hisses at the sight of my pussy stretched open by his thick length. Smirking, I raise up his cock again, sliding to the tip and dropping back down. The next groan from his lips is long and low. Muscular thighs tremble beneath me. We're both close and unlike earlier, I don't want him coming before me.

"Dalton," I beg, sliding a hand to my clit. He catches on, knocking my hand aside and watching me slide up and down his cock like it's his favorite show. It probably will be after this. Deft fingers make small, firm circles on my clit and I come apart on Dalton's cock with a choked cry. His hand falls away and his hips raise off the bed to roughly fuck me. Sliding my legs back beneath me and slumping forward, I go limp, letting him use my pussy until his groan fills my ear. His fingers spread my ass cheeks wide as he pistons his cock in and out of me. I can feel the jerk and twitches, letting me know he's releasing inside of me.

I'm too wrung out to care, blinking drowsily. When he's done thrusting through the aftershocks, powerful arms wrap around me and soft lips press a kiss to my forehead.

"Go back to sleep, my flower. Tomorrow will be a better morning," he murmurs in a hoarse voice. Smiling sleepily, I nod, closing my eyes. I never thought I'd comfortably fall asleep in a Lasher's arms after unpacking some of my childhood trauma.

Life certainly has a sick sense of humor.

MORNING AFTER

NATALIA

NINETEEN

Blinking open my eyes, vision blurring, for a moment I'm not sure where I am. An etched ceiling with flower patterns looks down at me, weak sunlight streaming in from the window behind my head. Sitting up, clutching the bed sheet to my naked breasts, I discover the spot next to me is empty.

Running a hand over the cool satin sheets, the events of the past forty-eight hours come rushing back, the kidnapping, the skinning of Jason, and… Dalton. Cheeks burning hot, I slide my body out of the bed, chancing a peek out of the window I failed to notice last night. My mouth falls open. An impressive wood line stretches behind the house.

I glance around the room with fresh eyes, combining it with the glimpses of the rest of the house that I've seen, painting a picture. Either whoever Dalton's foster parents are is well-off, or he's rich. My lips tilt down into a frown, walking toward the dresser. Of course, rich people get up to crazy shit when they're bored, like kidnapping and maiming.

Ghosting my fingers over the clothes spread out on top

of the wooden dresser, I cringe at the attached price tags. Only a psychopath pays five hundred dollars for jeans. A considerate psychopath, I amend, sliding them up my thick thighs. They fit like a glove, contouring to every curve. I hate wearing jeans because they're rarely tailored to women over a size ten. I didn't even have to jump to get the rough material over my butt.

A pair of nude ballet flats rests near a spot where the pile of clothes used to be and I applaud Dalton's thoughtfulness again after sliding them on. They fit perfectly. Blowing a breath, I eye my hair critically. The curls appear tangled and knotted, sticking to my scalp. Shaking my head, I remind myself I shouldn't care what Dalton thinks of my appearance, even if there is an ache between my thighs from how many times I let him fuck me last night.

A new day brings clarity.

Taking deep, even breaths, I stride from the bedroom in search of my psychopath.

Stepping down the last step of the curving black staircase, bacon teases my nose. A kitchen winks at me and through an open doorway, I spot a glimpse of blonde hair. Slowing my steps, I approach the kitchen on what I hope is silent feet, wishing to observe him unaware. Pausing in the open doorway, a smile teases my lips, a familiar tune being hummed floating to me.

It's a new dawn, it's a new day
It's a new life for me, ooh
And I'm feeling good

Snickering, I cover my smile, but he caught me,

piercing blue eyes ensnaring me. His smile stretches wide and he sets down the spatula, hurrying over to me. Telling my heart to calm down is useless, staring up into his eyes, his body crowding me into the frame of the doorway.

"Morning," he whispers before claiming my mouth, our tongues getting reacquainted. Pulling him to me, I let my fingers brush the shaved back of his head, soft fuzz brushing my palm. His groan echoes through my mouth before he pulls away.

"You look good in the clothes I picked out." Heat simmers in his eyes, but he pulls away, reaching for my hand, tugging me into the kitchen.

"Sit, my lady. I'll serve breakfast shortly, and I've got champagne and orange juice for mimosas," he says, winking at me. His good mood nearly infects me, my butt landing in a high-backed wooden chair.

I rest my cheek against my raised palm, watching him work, another pair of black jeans cupping his taut butt. A black shirt stretches across his muscled torso, sunlight kissing the brown tones in his sandy blonde hair.

My eyes travel to the tattoos that start below his fingernails and travel all the way up the peak of his shoulders. Garish bones etched into his skin, shaded in with black ink. In the dark, I'd probably mistake him for a walking skeleton, except for his face remaining blemish free. He'd even tattooed his neck. Mentally, I jot down "high pain tolerance", adding to my catalog of this strange man who's taken me hostage.

"Liking what you see?" he fires over his shoulder, not bothering to turn around, walking toward the silver fridge. I open my mouth to respond, words getting trapped when the fridge flies open, Jason's flayed skull judging me from its position on the top shelf next to the orange juice Dalton pulls out. Still humming, he reaches for the neighboring champagne, bile rising in my throat at spotting a second head.

Jumping to my feet, adrenaline rushing through me, I'm tempted to run. Dalton looks over at me, shutting the fridge closed with a boot covered foot.

"Where's the fire?" he jokes, smiling. I shake my head, nostrils flaring. I can't do this. It was dumb to consider I could.

"Natalia?" he asks, setting his items down, walking toward me. I jump back, a wall blocking my retreat.

"Woah!" His hands raise in the air placatingly, palms facing me.

"What the hell got into you?" I point at the fridge, tears rising up. He glances from it to me, eyebrows shooting up. After a moment, his face shuts down, dread tingling down my spine.

"I see," he says quietly, walking to turn the burners off, sliding eggs and bacon onto a plate. I wait, heart slamming against my ribs. Turning back slowly, hands fisting at his side, his jaw clenches and unclenches.

"So, this is the part where we get back to reality. Where you realize," his hand slaps his chest, "I haven't changed in the hours since I first put my dick inside of you." I flinch at the blunt words.

His eyes slide away from me, face etched in stone.

"Dalton," I whisper, uncertainty swimming among the dread. He shakes his head at me and I swear I see a glint of unshed tears.

"No, you're right. How idiotic of me to assume for a moment that someone cared about me. That last night meant something, that it was special." He doesn't meet my eyes and his words splinter into my heart.

"I need some air. Enjoy your breakfast or don't. I doubt you'll be here when I get back. At least give me a head-start before you call the cops." His defeated tone lances through me.

"Dalton—" But he's already striding away from me, boots slamming into the floor. Feeling worse than dog shit, I watch him leave, sliding to the floor, back against the wall.

How did this happen?

FIX IT

DALTON

TWENTY

Wind slams into me at one hundred and twenty miles an hour, hands clenched around the handles of my bike, Natalia's fear struck face taunting my mind.

How did I fuck this up so epically before it even began?

Getting up at the fucking ass crack of dawn, cleaning up the meat from the night before, buying her clothes and preparing breakfast, I thought for sure it'd win her over, convince her to stay. My hands kick the bike into higher gear, needing more speed to outrace the voices in my head.

You're a monster, a freak. We never should've adopted you. I'd take you back if I didn't think you'd kill the new fosters in their sleep. How would Charles and I live with each other if that happened? So, we're stuck with you.

"Fucking bitch!" I scream, turning sharply, body nearly brushing asphalt before the bike gets righted. I keep going, one destination in mind, the only place that doesn't make me feel ill in my own skin, ashamed of my needs.

Dick's Junkyard comes up and the ache in my chest eases only slightly, slowing the bike down until I'm parked in front of a chain-link fence. I'm wrenching the helmet off before my leg swings over the bike, tossing the helmet aside carelessly. Violence churns within me, begging for an outlet.

I shove the fence open, glaring at the cars stacked on top of each other, row after row, waiting to be deconstructed.

"I need to hit something," I say, not turning to face the man sitting to my left, a lit cigarette wafting smoke in my peripheral vision. A hand waves me forward, black nail polish catching the rays of sunlight.

"Have at it," he says in a bored tone. Deaton always sounds bored, as if he's seen all the mysteries life offered and wound up disappointed. At ten years older than me, maybe he has.

To my right rests a metal bat and it feels good wrapping my hand around it, boots kicking up dirt as I march toward the nearest piece of scrap.

Metal gleams and it pisses me off further, my arm pulling the bat back and swinging forward. Glass shattering sounds like music, light and whimsical. So I do it again and again. Jumping on the trunk, I smash the back windows in, jump onto the roof, slide down, and swing the bat into the windshield.

Jumping off the hood, I smash the bat down once I touch solid ground. Deaton doesn't speak a word, smoking while I vent out my anger and underlying disappointment.

Why couldn't it work out? Smash.
Am I really that different? Smash.
Is she really all that special? Smash.

Crumbling to my knees, tossing the bat aside, I know the answer to the last question. Yes, she is. No one has awakened within me the urges that she has. Only her skin tempts my lips and fingers, raising my cock from the land of limp dick.

"Woman trouble?" Deaton calls out, a mocking note entering his voice. Now he wants to chit chat. Annoying fucker. If we weren't one and the same, I'd have killed him years ago. But it was Deaton who'd taken me by the shoulder, putting a knife in my hand and gave voice to the urges churning within my blood. We respectfully hunt in separate grounds.

Dusting dirt off my jeans, I holler back, "How's Uncle Dick and Aunt Shirley?" I never see Dick around, it's always Deaton loitering when I need to come smash something into a million pieces. Demolishing scrap cars doesn't bring police to your door like leaving a pile of dead bodies does.

"Good, thinking of retiring early. He keeps saying he's getting too old for this shit but we all know I've been running the show for the past five years." Deaton's tone resorts to his usual chord of boredom. Walking over with a false smile, heart still aching, I wisely keep my mouth shut and not ask if he actually killed his dad, summoning some professional curtesy.

"What's with you?" he asks again, waving his cigarette at me.

"Nothing. What's with you? Not enough work for you to do around here?" My eyes twitch and I fight the urge to fidget. Small talk is my weakness. Just spit the shit out.

"You're not covered in blood and twitching like a damn drug addict so you're not hurting to kill something. So it can only mean you've got woman trouble. About time you got laid." He pulls a drag on the corpse maker. I wonder if he'd let me have his corpse if he kicks it.

"No trouble." I'm not taking relationship advice from a guy who told me to fuck an eye socket, that it was the best nut he ever had. Some things we just don't do. Pull the meat off and be done with it. Save the skull to jerk off with for later. The end.

Brown eyes narrow on me. I'm surprised he can see beneath the fucking mountain of eyeliner under his peepers. Or is it eye shadow? Weird fuck.

"Fine, but—" he points his cig again, "until you fix that shit, no more smashing my cars." My fingers twitch, imagining the dirt stained with his blood. He smiles knowingly.

"Fine. I have woman trouble. Are you happy? Can we skip the therapy sesh?" I turn to go, but his words halts me, wrapping around my limbs.

"Normies get a little squeamish, cous. And when they're squeamish, they get loose lips that tell the cops everything. Fix that shit or I'll fix it for you." Turning around, wishing the fucking bat was in my hand to bash his brains in, I notice he's already jumped to his feet, long dark hair flowing like a fucking cape around him.

Alright, Fabio. This is not a hair commercial.

Opening my mouth, he beats me to it. "I'm just saying, stabby hands, that if you go down, I go down, too. Is she a risk?" His chest moves rapidly up and down. So my little flower has him nervous, as if I can't pluck her again.

"She's not a risk," I lie, folding my arms, feigning nonchalance. The stink eye he gives me says enough. He's no fool.

"We're working things out," I amend.

"How? What did you do?" He drops the stub of a cigarette, squishing it beneath his leather combat boots. I don't comment on his fashion sense, but my tongue burns to say something. What did he ask me?

Snapping my fingers when the gist of the conversation returns to me, I debate lying again. What could it hurt? He'd probably tell me to fuck a corpse or something.

"She got a little upset over her ex's head being in my fridge," I grumble, eyes on the dirt. Maybe Uncle Dick can hire someone else if he's getting old. I wonder what Aunt Shirley is up to these days. She always made a damn good shepherd's pie.

"Zac!" Deaton snaps at me, face flushed red. "Are you shitting me right now? Did you fuck her?" My lips twist at having to admit something as private and special as what I shared with Natalia. I nod my head, looking away from his judgment.

He's breathing heavily, pacing away from me, mumbling under his breath. I fail to see the problem. It's not like she knows Deaton exists. Whirling on me, black hair flaring out, he points a finger painted black in my direction.

"Fix it and do not bring your ass around here until you do. I don't care how, just do it," he snarls, stalking toward the building a few feet away, looking like a goth kid's wet dream.

Fuck. Feeling resigned, albeit less murderous than moments before, I march back toward my motorcycle. Even if she's pissed and disgusted with me, my cock still twitches at seeing her again.

*P*ushing the door open, stepping into the house, I instantly know she's gone. Dread pools in my stomach and I race upstairs, boots pounding on the wood. Bursting into my empty bedroom, I resist screaming the fucking house down. She's not here and I don't need to search the whole fucking house to know it.

She left me. Just like I told her she could. What the fuck was I thinking?

"Nat," I whine, pausing when I notice a piece of paper on my nightstand. Rushing over, nearly tripping in my haste, I snatch it up, eyes scanning the contents quickly. The fuck?

> Dear Dalton,
> Please don't come looking for me. I'm not saying stay away forever, but I need some space, time to think. You have to know our situation is unusual. You kidnapped me and murdered my ex. I need time to process that and what happened between us the night before. I enjoyed every bit of it, you know I did. But, please, give me some space. You'll probably watch me anyways, but I'll signal when I'm ready to talk.
> Love, Natalia.

No. She can't do this. She—My thoughts freeze, tongue going numb. Space? What the fuck is space?

My butt sinks onto my mattress, brain frozen, unwilling to process Natalia's absence. My body hungers for her and she needs… space. I can do space, my head nodding as I think through the best ways to win her over. I don't even fucking care about finding my birth parents. All I want is Natalia, my little cacao flower.

Mine. Mine. Mine. Mine.

Count your fucking days, Natalia. Soon, you'll be back home, my flower. Soon.

SPACE

NATALIA

TWENTY ONE

A garish pink door stares at me, silently asking if I'll knock. I remember sitting on the hood of a car, sun beaming down on me in my denim shorts and tank top, a wine cooler in my hand, watching my eight-year-old niece paint, sloppily slinging it everywhere. Sarah and I giggled, content to let her have fun. We shared a smile and a knowing look.

Our parents never said it and neither did Sarah, but each time her test score surpassed mine or her report cards boasted more A's, I withdrew more and more. Leaving home for college was the most freeing thing I could've done.

Several shitty boyfriends and years of therapy later, Sarah and I reconciled, shedding the animosity of our youth, allowing her to open the door into her life with Lauren to me. I never appreciated it more until now. Before I lose my nerve, my knuckles rap on the door, anxiously waiting for my little sister to open the door for me again. I wouldn't blame her if she didn't after the last thing I said.

It eases open cautiously, a wary Sarah running shrewd eyes up and down my frame.

"I'm sorry," I blurt, tears clogging my throat. Wordlessly, she throws the door open and pulls me into a hug.

All the emotions of the past forty-eight hours race to the surface and I sag against her, letting out wrenching sobs, body shaking with the force of my tears. I missed my sister, tightening my grip on her. It was a stupid, selfish thing for me to say the last time I spoke to her and pales compared to everything I've experienced lately.

I needed this, inhaling her sweet vanilla scent, letting it calm me, nostalgia welling up. Sarah has used the same shampoo since the day our mother let us start picking out our own hair products.

It grounds me. Why couldn't figuring things out with Dalton be this easy?

*R*ed liquid swirls, hypnotizing me.

"Are you going to drink it or make love to it?" Sarah jokes from across the room, seated in the dark-haired man's lap she introduced as Zaiden. Another Lasher. I overheard her call him Dayton while pouring me a glass of wine, but maybe that's something shared between just the two of them.

Bringing the glass to my lips, I gulp it down, needing the potent liquid to relax my muscles and reassure me my life isn't about to implode any further.

"The man that took you, are you sure Dalton is his name?" Zaiden asks, rubbing a palm up and down Sarah's back. Glancing at his face makes me wince, the scars sending phantom pain spreading across my own face. At least two-inch scars stretch from the sides of his mouth to nearly his earlobe. I don't want to know who inflicted those.

I nod at his question, but how certain can I be? He's a killer.

"And his mother is Morgan Daniels?" Zaiden presses again and I'm tempted to rise from the sofa and smack him for the constant questions. Yes, you have a brother and he's a homicidal psychopath.

That can fuck like a pornstar despite being a damn virgin. Down, kitty, I chastise my libido.

"Are you sure he won't come here looking for you?" Sarah asks, a hint of worry in her voice. Dammit. I hope I haven't endangered them. All I can do is hope on a wish that Dalton respects my request for space.

"I can't be sure, Sarah. He kidnapped me once. It's not outside the realm of possibilities that he'd do it again." Wincing at my tone coming out harsher than I intended, I open my mouth, but she waves me away with a hand.

"Alright, you can have Lauren's old room. Or sleep on the sofa if it's more comfortable," she says, ending the interrogation. My eyes dart between her and Zaiden, wondering if she told him yet and if I'll have to listen to my sister getting dicked down while hiding out from the man who gave me the best sex of my life.

How fucking ironic is my life right now?

DALTON

Two days. Two fucking days is how long it takes to break me. I can't take it anymore, glaring down into the chest cavity of ex number five. How many dicks did my girl fuck in her lifetime? It took a deep dive down her social media to find the five pricks I did.

Scowling, I tug my gloves off, tossing them into a wastebasket, leaning against the slab. This latest excavation leaves me unfulfilled. As did the other four, swinging from hooks I'd drilled into the ceiling out of boredom.

A steady drip, drip, drip bounces around the room, some of them still leaking blood into pails stationed beneath their arms. I hung them feet up, digging hooks into their rib cages, attached to a length of chain and attaching that to the hooks in the ceiling. They died hours ago, but I couldn't decide what I wanted as a trophy.

A waste of meat. It's all Natalia's fault. Before her, I wasted nothing. Fuck this. I'm going to get my girl, even if I have to drag her kicking and screaming from Raven and Joke face.

As predicted, I tracked my flower the same day she left me while respecting her space, watching her come and go from her sister's house. Joker kept scanning the neighborhood, eyes sweeping up and down, but fuck you, novice. This was not my first stalking, but it will be my last. There's only one person I want to kidnap, and she fucking left me.

That was two days ago and I can't take anymore of this *space*. Maybe because they were too scared of what I'd do to them, but no one asked for space from me. No, they just ran as soon as they saw me coming, calling on whatever deity they worship, piss leaking down their legs. At least my flower hadn't pissed herself that first night I took her.

Giving Natalia's dead ex one smack across the face for good measure, I turn on a heel. Uncaring of the mess I leave behind, I stalk out of my playroom, pounding up the stairs and striding straight for the front door and my motorcycle. Natalia is coming home or my name isn't Zachary.

Dead fucker. I looked up his obituary, and he'd already kicked the bucket at the hands of a Xavier Lasher. How dumb are you to let your own kid kill you? Well, I guess as dumb as Samantha. I bet she didn't see that blade coming.

I think I'll like Xavier as soon as he gets over me kidnapping his girlfriend's aunt. Water under the bridge, bro. As Elsa said, let it fucking go.

One thing I'm not letting go is Natalia. Here I come, baby.

CLAIMING ZAIDEN

SARAH

TWENTY TWO

A warm weight presses into my chest. Soft, gentle breaths kiss my skin. Silky curls caress the fingers I run up and down a small head. My lips curl into the baby smooth skin beneath my lips as I inhale my child's fresh scent.

"Sarah!" Jostling shakes loose the pleasant cocoon of the dream I was enjoying. A dark blob floats above me as I slowly blink open my eyes. Natalia's pinched face lazily blooms into focus.

"Sarah, wake up," she whispers urgently, sending warning bells ringing in my head. I jump upright, nearly colliding with her bent over torso. She jumps back with a relieved sigh. Jerking my head to the right, I note the empty spot in the bed next to me.

I turn wide eyes back onto my sister. "Where's Day—Zaiden? Is your guy here?" I climb out of bed as the words leave my lips in a rush. Worry sinks into the pit of my stomach. If Zaiden and Zachary were to meet… A shudder runs through me at the ramifications of them killing each other.

"No, Dalton isn't here. But Zaiden is downstairs," Nat whispers, wringing her hands in front of the borrowed shirt that falls to her knees. It's one of Zaiden's and I'd had to push aside a twinge of jealousy at having to hand it over for her to sleep in.

My brows drop low as her words penetrate my sleep fogged brain. Zaiden's downstairs? But—My lips drop open and my eyes widen, hurrying out of the bedroom with Nat quickly padding behind me, feet slapping the hardwood floors.

Leaning over the bannister of the second floor, I listen for his gravelly voice. It floats to me and it sounds like he's holding a conversation with someone but only his voice reaches my ears.

The darkened living room looks empty from my vantage point, no shadowed shapes moving around below me. His voice must be carrying from the kitchen. I move to step down the stairs but a hand landing on my arms forces me to pause and look at my sister's frightened eyes.

"Sarah," she pleads, nails slightly denting my skin. "Are you sure this is—"

"He's mine," I nearly snarl, ripping my arm free. I don't need her to finish her sentence. Zaiden's mine just as I'm his. And I'll drag him from the hells of his mind each and every time to remind him who he belongs to. His demons can't have him.

"Go to bed, Nat." I gentle my voice so it doesn't sound quite like an order but the steel in my tone closes the door on the discussion of Zaiden's mental health. I know what I signed up for.

Wood creaks beneath my bare feet as I tiptoe down the stairs. Zaiden's probably in the middle of an episode, and the last thing I want is to startle him. A light illuminates Zaiden's naked back. Gray pajama pants hang low on his hips. I approach cautiously, picking up bits and pieces of his side of the imagined conversation.

"Do you like that?"

"What about Sarah?"

"Oh, really? You're happy?"

His whispered gravel voice gets stronger the closer I get to the kitchen until I'm leaning against the doorframe. His back still faces me and he keeps whispering to the hallucination sitting across from him. He sits on a stool, one arm resting on the island and body tilted toward the empty seat next to him, as if he's listening to the other half of the conversation.

Suddenly, his back straightens and he hops off the stool, whirling to face me with a guilty expression, ears turning red.

He pants, darting blue eyes from the empty seat and back to me.

"Sarah—" He waves his hand at the seat without offering more of an explanation. A flush stains his cheeks and broad shoulders tilt forward, shrinking. Nausea swims in my gut and it's not because of the pregnancy. I hate seeing him like this, folding in as if anticipating a rebuke or a physical assault.

"Dayton," I say, keeping my voice gentle, imitating his whispered voice from a few moments ago. My arms lift, beckoning him forward. Cautiously, he takes one step toward me, unfocused eyes glancing around the kitchen, looking for an escape or a trap to close around him. He does this with each lift and fall of his large, bare feet until his face looms above me, inches away.

A minute flinch ripples across his skin as I lift my hand to rest on his cheek. He remains tense for several moments before relaxing into the touch, eyes drifting closed. Full lips part, allowing deep inhales and exhales. We stay like that, letting the silence press on us as he wrestles with his mind.

"Sarah," he croaks, bringing a hand to my waist and pulling me closer. Breath brush over my face.

"We have a son," he whispers, eyes staying closed. His tongue slips out, wetting his lips. "We name him Zade." My lip trembles and tears spring to my eyes.

"That's nice." My voice crawls out around a rock that lodged in my throat. I pull his hand from my waist to my stomach, pressing it there and hoping it anchors him, reminding him that our child hasn't been born yet.

"I like that name," I tell him. His eyes pop open and a tentative smile curls his lips.

"Yeah?" I nod vigorously, feeling a stray tear trail down my cheek. He brushes a finger along my face, wiping the tears away.

"I'm sorry." I shake my head.

"Don't you dare apologize to me," I mock growl and he laughs nervously. "You have nothing to be sorry for. Your mind is simply telling you in its own special way what I already know. You're going to be an amazing father." More tears leak free and he wipes them away, his smile faltering.

"My Sarah," he croaks, bringing his forehead to rest against mine. "I love you," he says softly, like a confession.

I choke out a laugh, letting the tears fall freely now.

"I love you, too." My lips wobble, but I still bring them to brush along his and he eliminates all the space between our bodies. My fingers rake up and down his nape, reminding me of my dream. Was it a boy I held in my arms?

I don't know, and I don't care. I'm already holding the center of my universe. Anything else is a bonus.

FINDING FAMILY

DALTON

TWENTY THREE

That is a hideous color of pink. It's like Barbie threw up on the door. Who thought this was a good idea? Grimacing and prancing in place, I try to hype myself up. I can do this. She'll be happy to see me. I'm the marshmallow to her hot chocolate. A better duo than Peanut Butter and Jelly.

Nodding, blood rushing, I tap my knuckles to the door in quick succession three times. If she opens the door and slams it in my face, I'll just come back when everyone is sleeping and snatch her up like I did last time. Space. It's a stupid idea.

The door swings open, and I gawk at Joker. That probably isn't his name, but with those scars sitting on either side of his mouth, it should be. Dark hair brushes his forehead, the shaved sides a little too similar to my own hair cut. Blinking, I think back to Natalia telling me this guy was a Lasher, another son of my father's business partner. I guess that makes us brothers.

If he's standing in my way, keeping me from Natalia, then he's about to be a dead brother.

"Is Nat here?" I ask, unable to see around his bulky frame. He doesn't speak, stepping back and pulling the door open wider. Giving him an appreciative nod, I step through, scanning the living room for my flower and coming up empty. Two fucks I don't know sit on sofas on opposite sides of the room.

The one to my left sits on the sofa against the wall nearest the door, a dark-haired babe clutched in his arms. He runs assessing blue eyes over me, but I couldn't care less about his opinion, glancing at the dark-haired fucker on the other sofa. His solemn expression matches the other one.

If I didn't know any better, someone was getting an intervention, and I didn't sign up for one.

"Where's my girl?" I ask, fury rising and my knives pleading in wheezy voices for me to kill them all.

"She's with her sister," Joker chimes in, arms folded across his muscled chest, crossing his ankles while leaning against the door. Well, exit one is now blocked.

"My Zoe is with her too. Apparently you fucked up, and she needs cheering up," the blonde speaks up, rocking back and forth, jostling the infant a little in between rocks. What a waste of time. And my business with Natalia is none of theirs.

Opening my mouth, the other dark-haired member of the trio speaks up, cutting me off.

"I'm Xander. The grumpy blonde is Zaine, and that's Zaiden at the door. I'm your cousin and they're your brothers," he says, eyes trying to peer into my soul. Swallowing, I try to think through what I want to say.

First, I want to say get bent, but I don't think that'll go over well if they're anything like me and Deaton.

Second, who's fucking child is Zaine rocking? It better not be Natalia's or I'm killing someone today. Well, someone else, remembering ex number five from a little while ago.

"I'm Zachary. So this is the circle jerk going on while the women are away?" I ask, going for deflection. Zaine's lips thin and he rises, nostrils flaring and glaring at me.

"Why should we let you anywhere near Natalia?" Zaine asks, getting to the point. He keeps going, "Hmm? You kidnapped her, killed her ex, and frightened the fuck out of her. She's the aunt to my future sister-in-law, so Xavier and I don't have a fucking problem putting you six feet under. We got him." His head jerks at Zaiden.

So that's how it is. I step forward until the tips of my shoes knock against the tips of his.

"Let me make myself clear then, brother. I also don't have a fucking problem putting any of you six feet under, so I suggest you mind your own damn business unless you're looking to lose someone precious to you," I snarl. Rustling to my left has my eyes snapping to Xander.

He scowls at me and Zaine, snapping, "Put your damn dicks away. You're brothers, for fuck's sake. We all care for Natalia," he looks at me meaningfully. "If you want to make sure she doesn't run scared from you again, maybe take some damn advice from those in the room who also kidnapped their girlfriends." My eyebrows raise at that, swinging my eyes to meet Zaine's gaze.

A light pink blush stains his cheeks and cupping the little girl with one arm, he flips Xander the middle finger with the other before sitting back down.

Patting the babe's bottom—I'm assuming she's his damn kid—with one hand and resuming his rocking, he asks me, "So how are you going to win her over? Zaiden had flowers, but he didn't peel the skin from Sarah's ex."

I don't regret that one bit, but I don't volunteer the information that I killed her prior five exes.

"Fine. What do you suggest?" My hands snake into my back pockets, rocking on my heels as I await their suggestions.

Zaine's lips curl up, and I immediately hate whatever he's about to say. "You can promise not to kill indiscriminately. Maybe even make a date night out of it. Go to a club, prowl for would-be rapists trying to drug some girl's drink. You can use her as bait. You get a kill and she gets a clean conscience for ridding the world of scum."

Grumbling under my breath, I admit that's not a terrible idea. I could do that, become a reformed killer for my flower. Sighing and resigning myself to being a kept man, I jerk my chin at the beer resting at Xander's feet.

"You got any more of those?" I ask. Zaine snorts and Xander gets up, walking toward the kitchen through the doorless archway at the back of the room. If it doesn't have doors, does that make it an open floor plan? I bet Samantha would know.

"So, what do you do?" Zaiden asks, walking toward Zaine and taking a seat. I don't answer, watching Zaine carefully transfer the bundle into my other brother's waiting hands, smitten looks on both of their faces. Xander walks back in with the beer and I take it gratefully, turning my back on the father duo.

"Not a fan of kids, I see," Xander quips, paying closer attention than my brothers. Shaking my head, pulling out a knife to pop the cap off of the beer, I gulp it down greedily once I have access to the precious liquid.

After about five minutes, silently pacing, beer in hand, my skin is close to crawling off me with boredom.

"Why don't you chill?" Xander pipes up again, making me want to rearrange his teeth. What is up with these freaks? Everything is too normal, my stomach twisting nauseously. I spot Zaine getting up and I'm fucking ready, tossing the empty beer bottle to the floor after draining the last bit.

He just stares at me, brow cocked. I don't like how similar we look. I don't like the baby's cute little babble erupting from her while Uncle Zaiden holds her. And I fucking can't stand the normalcy of drinking beer while the women are out doing God knows what.

Zaine sees too much and I'm jumping back when he prowls closer, all lithe muscles shifting, reminding me too much of a lion preparing to pounce. And I feel like the fucking gazelle. My breathing is coming fast and I don't know how to slow it, palms sweating. What the fuck is wrong with me?

Hands touch me and I lash out, but I'm shoved roughly against a wall, a hard forehead thunking into mine. Zaine breathes with me, one hand pressed on my throat and the other pinning a shoulder to the wall.

"Who's in your head, Z?" I shake it emphatically, but I swear I *hear* her, whispering how I'm an abomination, that I don't deserve a fucking family. Is she right?

"No," Zaine says, answering the question I don't remember opening my mouth to ask. "She's wrong and she never should've told a child that. You have issues, we all do. But I've got you. I'm your big brother and I'm right fucking here. This is what family is. We pick up the pieces when your arms are too damn heavy. Let it go, Z."

My knees buckle and Zaine catches me, tearless sobs leaving me, stretching that wound I didn't know I had wide fucking open, letting all the pain and fear out.

She's dead. She's dead. She's dead. I did that. I killed her. I plucked Natalia up, the only lead to my family. Zaine rocks us and I let him, eyes drifting closed. Deaton never held me like this and being so tightly wound, I don't think I would've let him.

It took witnessing my two brothers fawn over an infant to realize how deeply I craved that. Not a kid, but family, that easy fucking connection that I never had with the Lewis'. Zaine keeps holding me, waiting for me to signal I'm ready to let go. I don't think I'll ever be willing to let go of this feeling. It feels too much like coming home.

NATALIA

My feet ache from endless walking through the mall, but my cheeks hurt from all the smiling. A girls' day was exactly what the doctor ordered, and it felt wonderful. Zoe and Sarah chatted frequently about pregnancy, lactating and the price of formula going up while I talked about anything and everything between the two women.

Sarah and I frequently made trips down memory lane. Zoe and I got more acquainted, swapping experiences between us, from finding the right leave-in conditioner to discussing some of the blatant racism we experienced in the workplace. It felt good, too good, placing a balm on the festering hole left behind by Dalton.

Pulling into the driveway of Sarah's house, looking out of the window, I'm loath for the day to end. I'm not looking forward to saying goodnight to Sarah and goodbye to Zoe, whose fiancé is eager to place her back under mock house arrest. Before we left, I noted the possessive aura pulsing around Zaine and Zaiden, each snagging an arm around their woman, poking at the Dalton sized hole. It's clear they're over the moon for the two women.

But I remind myself that great sex does not make a

great relationship, especially when one is a killer. Stepping out of the car, my eyes snag on a motorcycle parked near the sunroom's window.

I look at Sarah, walking around the car and point at the unknown vehicle. "Whose is that?" She shrugs, jerking her head toward the door. My heart rate picks up, my body sensing exactly who the bike belongs to, panties growing wetter with each step toward the pink door.

Sarah opens it, Zoe trailing behind us, and laughter slips through the doorframe. We step through and gawk at the men in the living room. All four of them sit around the coffee table, each holding a hand of playing cards, Zaria resting near Zaine's leg in a car seat he rocks absently with one hand.

I've stepped into an alternate universe. Dalton sets his cards down, the laughter dying down now that they've noticed us. He looks good, still wearing all black like the color is going out of style.

"Can we talk? In private?" His head jerks at the kitchen entryway. Several pairs of eyes jump around the room, avoiding us. I nod, too shocked to do anything. This was not what I had expected to come home to. He smiles, arming himself with those dimples, and holds out a hand.

A gravitational pull yanks me toward him until our fingers link and he's leading me into the kitchen.

MY FLOWER

DALTON

TWENTY FOUR

Her hand feels good in mine. I'm reluctant to release it when we enter the open space of the kitchen, but I don't fight it when she slips from my grip, pacing away from me. Wiping my palms on my pants, I decide to rip the band-aid off.

"Natalia," I murmur, waiting for her to turn around. Before I can say the speech I've been repeating in my head, she talks over me, brown eyes sparking with anger, holding a glossy sheen of tears.

"What are you doing here, Dalton? I asked for space. This isn't space." Her hand waves at the room behind me, where I just know my fucking brothers are eavesdropping. She's not exactly whispering, putting this whole spectacle on display.

Is this what she wants or needs to feel safe with me?

"I know." Nodding my head, I inhale deeply, reaching deep for humility, scraping the bottom of the fucking well, because this is hard.

"I couldn't stay away." I walk toward her, slowly, watching her pupils expand. "I can't stay away from you,

Nat. I need you, probably more than I need to kill." Another deep inhale, slow on the exhale. "I'm willing to change, to try and be what you need," I confess, heart in my throat.

The power to destroy me rests in her fucking palms.

"I just got out of a relationship, Dalton. You'd know, apparently you stalked me and witnessed the whole thing. And you killed him." She sniffs and I wish I could kill him all over again for bringing tears to my flower's eyes.

"He didn't deserve you—"

"And you do?" she snaps, but doesn't back away when I eliminate the space between us, wanting to share the same oxygen as her.

"No." my head shakes. "I don't deserve you. And my brain is so fucked up, but Nat, I'll do anything to keep that smile on your face. When you smile, it's like the fucking sun comes out, warming me on the inside." Her mouth drops open and I keep going.

"I didn't know it, but you mesmerized me from the first moment I saw you, captivating me. When I stood in your bedroom, and saw he didn't appreciate the fucking gift he had, I decided to kill him, not knowing my reasons were purely selfish. He had you and threw it away on some fucking bimbo."

My flower stares up at me, wide-eyed, mouth held open as I keep going, completely forgetting the speech I prepared.

"I can't and won't promise that I won't fuck up. I will. But I'm willing to do any damn thing for you." My hands come up to grip her neck, and she lets me, her breath fanning my lips.

"Anything, but let you go. If you want more space, fine, but know I'll probably camp out on the lawn just to be close to you." She laughs, a stray tear falling down her cheek.

"All I'm asking for is a chance. An itty bitty, little chance. Give me that and I'll try to give you the fucking world." I wait, staring into the eyes of the woman who's becoming my universe.

One blink, and more tears escape her eyes.

"Thirty days." She swallows against the thumbs brushing up and down her throat. "Thirty days, Dalton. Convince me in thirty days and I'm yours." I yank her forward, our mouths crashing together, tongues tangling, and I've never been happier.

This. I'd fucking kill to keep all of this. And I will. Pulling away, something moves in my peripheral and I turn in time to spot Zaine giving me a thumbs up and a wink, an arm curled around his woman, who gazes lovingly down at their child clutched in her arms.

This is my family, and I am so fucking happy to have found them.

EPILOGUE

DEATON

EPILOGUE

This is stupid. And boring. Music pumps through the speakers of the club, blood filled bodies gyrating on the dance floor. Condensation wets my hands, lifting the glass of whiskey to my lips. I hate that I let Dalton sweet talk me into coming along for his "date" night.

The whiskey burns on the way down, my eyes finding Dalton sitting in a darkened corner of the club, blue eyes frequently reflecting the strobe lights. I follow his gaze to his woman sitting a few chairs down from me at the bar, a backless gown showing off her toffee skin. I like the way her skin holds the light, giving none of it back, a beautiful blank canvas. It's too bad Dalton is over the moon about her.

It's still stupid to even pretend to share, both of them hunting for prey with Natalia as bait. My eyes sweep the sheep in the building, but nothing grabs my attention. I drain the last of my drink, standing to leave, but pausing when I notice a blonde man walking up to my future cousin in law. He chats with her, a false smile twisting his lips.

But it's the man who's been sitting next to her for the past hour drawing my predatory gaze. While she's distracted with the blonde, he leans, sprinkling a powdery solution into her drink. My head swivels to Dalton, who's already cutting a path through the crowd. Well, this is about to get interesting, I think, retaking my seat.

I truly enjoy watching my cousin work, a true protégé. Remorse over Aunt Samantha's death never arose upon hearing about her "accident." Eyes riveted to Dalton stalking through the crowd, my instincts scream at me her death was no accident, that I trained a killer.

Good. The world is too populated, anyway. Someone needs to thin the herd.

NATALIA

My nipples bead with excitement, adrenaline surging through my veins. Who the fuck knew I'd get off on this? Stranger Danger sitting next to me gave off creep vibes from the moment he sidled next to me, trying to make idle conversation. I don't doubt he's attempting to tamper with my drink as Mr. Corporate tries to butter me up.

His green gaze keeps wandering down to the deep V of my gown, his attention drawn to all the skin on display, a hint of the curve of my breasts acting as a flashing sign.

"I own a condo not far from here if you want to go somewhere quiet—" He stills before slowly turning to Dalton, a shark-like grin on my man's handsome face. I can't see through the press of their bodies, but I'm sure he has a blade pressed to the spine of Mr. Corporate.

"I don't think she wants to go anywhere with you, so run along before this gets messy." Dalton's voice slides over me, teasing my skin. He's blown my world wide open during the thirty-day deadline I gave him, from edging me in public, a toy nestled within my pussy that he controls, to arriving bright and early to Sarah's, waking me to his tongue between my legs.

Zaiden had the bright idea of gifting his twin a key, and Dalton took advantage while the couple slept. I spent the past thirty days there, strengthening my bond with Sarah, signing up for coaching classes with her on days Zaiden had work, shopping for baby clothes and everything in between. It's scary how good things have been going and Dalton's eyes promise it'll only get better, stepping back and allowing his prey to scamper away.

"You look fucking delectable, my flower," he says, coming closer and ghosting his lips across mine, but I know he's spotted the creep oby the side of me.

"I'll be right back, baby. I won't be far," he whispers, heat simmering in his eyes, filled with sinful promises. I watch him stalk away, disappearing into the crowd.

DALTON

My cock has never been this hard in my life. Natalia looks like a damn meal I can't wait to devour and for once, it's not actual flesh I'm craving to feast on, her pussy becoming my favorite meal.

Thirty days of hell is what I called it. Tonight marks the day after her deadline, the night she'll say yes to being mine and I couldn't think of anything better than reminding her of what she's getting into bed with, taking Zaine's suggestion.

Deaton's eyes track me, a dark caress I can feel. He always enjoyed stepping back and watching me work. I invited him for sentimental purposes, a sort of graduation, a transfer of ownership. After tonight, Natalia owns me and I her. This'll mark the end of the rare hunts I shared with Deaton. My flower will be my master, her dainty hands leading me to my next kill.

The scum sitting next to her keeps lavishing leery looks on her derriere. The first thing I'll take is his eyes. Then his tongue so he can never speak to my flower. Growing impatient, as his ilk is prone to do, he gets up, heading in the direction of the men's bathroom.

Bingo. It's playtime.

Stalking my prey in the overcrowded club, sweat slicked bodies bumping against one another, is too damn easy. Eyes tracking my bounty, I pull my phone out, shooting a quick text to Natalia.

> Meet me in the men's bathroom.

How fortunate for us there isn't a line. The meat bag makes it in before me and I soon follow, thanking my lucky stars that we're the only occupants. His eyes find mine, a question in them before he darts them back down into the urinal, zipper sounding louder in the muted room.

I disappear into a stall, piss and unpleasant scents assaulting my nose. In my other pocket lies pieces of a blow dart that I quickly assemble, peeking through the crack to make sure my prey doesn't wander off. It's pressed to my lips, ready for my breath to shoot the paralytic through the crack into the meat of the idiot who thought it was a good idea to violate my flower.

The bathroom door flies open and I know it's her, cock twitching in my pants.

"What the hell—" My catch of the day startles. I yank the door open and blow, watching it hit its mark.

"Lock the door," I command Natalia, hurrying to catch my prey before the thud of his body hitting the floor draws attention. I slid him beneath the base of the urinals, kneeling to begin working.

"Dalton," Natalia breathes. Her eyes prickle my skin as I drive the blade of one of my favorite knives into the eye socket of her would-be attacker, scraping along the wall until the eye floats freely.

"Ugh," she says, feet darting into a stall, but I keep working, removing both eyes. What else did I say I'd take? Oh, his tongue, so he can't speak about this. What's the saying? See no evil, speak no evil. His body jerks occasionally, but mostly, he's paralyzed. I bet this is how his victims feel. Helpless, unable to fight back. It's bitter sweet poetic fucking justice.

Liquid splashes into one of the toilets and I pocket my trophies, walking in on Natalia vomiting. Fuck. I didn't think I could fuck this up.

"Nat." She shakes her head, silencing me. I wait until she's done, hoping this isn't the end of us. She stands, cocking a brow at my gloved hands. Did she think I'd risk us getting caught?

"Nat," I whisper, prowling closer and she moves until her bare back presses against the wall of the stall. My hand lands near her head, my eyes asking a silent question. She nods, hiking her dress up. Oh, fuck. I thought I'd scared her off.

"He deserved it," she answers my unspoken question. "That doesn't mean I'm used to the sight of blood and viscera." Her hands tug at the waistband of my pants, fingers quickly free my hard cock. Oh shit. This is happening. I'm about to fuck my flower in a bathroom stall with loose eyeballs squished in my pockets.

This night cannot get any better—a knock ends that thought. Scowling, refusing to tuck myself away, I march toward the door, opening it enough so to expose only my unzipped pants and a sliver of torso.

Deaton cocks a brow, and smiling, I let him, motioning at the body. It's all his. He walks in silently, jerking his head for me to lock the door. Natalia peeks through the stall and I was so unequivocally wrong. This night *could* get better.

Crooking a finger at her, I shove my pants down the rest of the way, cock completely exposed. She licks her lips nervously, darting frequent glances at Deaton, walking over. I ignore him, slamming her against the wall as soon as she's within touching distance.

This—not fucking a damn eye socket—is about to be the best nut of my life.

ABOUT THE AUTHOR

Mae K. Knight is an emerging author of dark and taboo romances.

She lives in Louisiana and can be found studying for her nursing degree or powerlifting when she's not dreaming up stories. She believes she has a morbid sense of humor and tries to incorporate this into her writing

Her books will take you on a wild ride you never asked to embark on. Buckle up. If you like your twisted romances with a dash of taboo, you've arrived at the right place. Enter Knight's den of inequity. Only the depraved enter and the brave leave...

Milton Keynes UK
Ingram Content Group UK Ltd.
UKHW021642011224
451755UK00011B/759